Chapter 1

I had just finished compiling my tea

We were all drained, weary and mal   ...o years
we had been on this case and finally....we had caught him. The villain
who had terrorised our lives for years. He was now in a cold iron cell.
Awaiting his fate.

That was when the call came in.

"Ma'am, we've got one!" The sergeant called through my open door, his
lined face already pulling on his coat.

I glanced at my second-handwristwatch. It was three forty am. I sighed
and rubbed my eyes, calling out as I got wearily to my feet. "Where?"

"Whitechapel!" An ominous reply. I pondered this as I pulled on my coat
and checked that my badge was on my belt. I knew the area well. The
East End of London. My ancestor chased and hunted killers and thieves.

My name was Margaret 'Maggie' Abberline. And I too lived in the East
End of London. Due to several unfortunate mishaps that always occur in
my family, my situation being slightly better off, even for a woman.
Living there was like being in a Dicken's novel. Even today it was still
known as the slums of London.

I grabbed my gun and slipped it into my holder as I followed my
sergeant out of the station, him falling to walking beside me as we
slipped into an unmarked police car.

As we sat there in companionable silence, I looked back at to our
beginning. We had, had problems when I had first arrived as a Detective
Inspector. He had been against the idea of having a woman, an old-
fashioned view, being in charge on a police force. But his view soon
changed as I defended him against an assailant that had tried to stab us
both in a mugging and handcuffed him in minutes without any backup.
That had earned his respect.

I remembered that day very well as we drove to the scene of the crime. I had been newly transferred almost a rookie from the beginning, and we had instantly hated each other on the spot. He liked his way done methodically, whereas I would jot things down as things came to me. We had been on the case for about a month, he was always removing information from whiteboards, refused to take me to crime scenes with him, even though he was supposed to. And on one night where we had, had very little sleep we ended up having the argument in the area where we were supposed to catch our suspect. He had told me "I never wanted a woman on the team-all you do is bring nothing but trouble!" It led to the suspect getting away, even though we had both given pursuit. From that point we had decided to not work against each other but not work with one another. The day of the capture came, and the suspect decided that he was going to run, I gave chase as soon as I saw him. Sergeant followed as best he could, handcuffs at the ready. But I had been quicker, despite a gun and a knife thrown at me, I had managed to jump out of the way of the bullets and the knife, handcuffs had been snapped on, I had begun reading him his rights as the sergeant arrived on the scene. No back up just a lowly woman. Things changed from then on. He began to ask for my opinion, asked for my notes so he could put them on the white boards, always asked if there was anything else to add and didn't remove anything. He also waited for me to go to crime scenes. Respect had been earned, but respect was easily taken away.

The scene of the crime...

We had reached the body. As I looked down at it, the yellow tape, famous in these parts flapped in the wind, seeing it out of the corner of my eye. We were in a cordoned off area. Private apart from those that lived there, my team and journalists already sticking their noses in to grab a good story.

Durward Street, 31st August.

That was today's date.

A shiver ran down my spine, someone clearly had walked over my grave. My bloodline was already telling me something. And my stomach lurched.

The body was of a woman. Covered now in a black plastic sheet due to forensics were discovering the cause of death.

My team was already hard at work, despite them not having seen their loved ones or eaten a decent meal for quite some time. I was extremely proud of them; their professionalism was something that I never took for granted.

I stood staring at that black plastic sheet. Wondering, was this how he felt? Did he feel as I did? Did he know that this would be the beginning? Surely, he couldn't have. That was a thought that had more than likely never crossed his mind. Lost in thought I vaguely heard the youngest of my team, but no means less experienced, sprint over to me, a steaming black coffee clutched in his hand like the Holy Grail itself.

"Thought you may need this Mags." He smiled. I allowed them all to call me Maggie, even when we were on duty, I hated being called Ma'am. But it was a respect thing in the police force and I never questioned it when we were outside. I thanked him and smiled weakly.

I inhaled the bitter and rich aroma of the coffee beans.

"What have you found out?" I asked him taking a sip.

"No witnesses. The man who found the body said she was cold when he found her, he was on his way home after a long shift, coming from the other side of London."

"Did he call for help?"

"Rang 999 straight away."

I thought for a moment. "Jack." Ironic. I thought. "Jack, now this may open a can of worms, but look into anything that may have happened in history on this date, look for anything like this. Just in case we have a serial killer. At least then we can justify why we have looked. Call it a hunch."

Jack, my youngest team member smiled. "Sure, thing Mags Ma'am, the press is already taking pictures so it will already be public."

"Damn it." I followed his pointed gaze that was on the press taking photographs for their latest story. "Make sure everyone tells them no comment until we find out more."

"Sure, will Mags Ma'am." He scampered off. I knew my team would tell them no comment. Their professionalism after all was everything I wished for in a team.

I walked back to the plastic bag. Already the past was beginning to haunt me. It always did when it came to my family. We could never catch a break.

Forensics had taken photographs and were moving the body back to the morgue at the police station.

The sergeant and I walked back to the car. The puzzle was to begin soon.

And sometimes I really hated puzzles.

I always found waiting for autopsy results a nail-biting experience. Even when I had first started out. It was a puzzle, sometimes I loved a puzzle, but I feared this one. Puzzles always helped the brain cells to connect, even when you haven't had time to recuperate. While we waited, we were ringing local businesses, the woman had been found on a street. An ordinary, everyday street. Our job was to find out who she was, looking through missing person's files, searching for who this poor woman could be.

While my team was on that side of this case, I was puzzling over the witness statement from the man who discovered the body. It was an agonising puzzle. Nothing was coherent. But then again, the witness had admitted to being drunk after the statement had been taken.

It would be no help to us. I removed my reading glasses and leaned back in my chair, thumbs going to my temple to ease the headache that had begun to appear. I blamed the lack of sleep and food. I glanced down at my watch.

Eight am. I should order in breakfast for the team. So, I did just that.

Wasn't long before our breakfast arrived and I heard the cheers of the team, who set a side a table that wasn't being used as a station.

"Thanks Ma'am." Johnathon said, grabbing a paper plate and putting a croissant and a pancake there so he could continue working but eat at the same time.

"Thanks Mags." The sergeant added. "You didn't have to do this." I could tell he was grateful though.

"Most of us have been working since last night. Not all of us have been able to go home. Food is good for morale." I simply stated. It was the truth. Many of us had been working overtime already. I knew Sergeant Jeffries;the Sergeant hadn't seen his children since yesterday morning when he had seen them off to school. His wife Ann had been in contact to let him know that they were with her mother, so she could go to work. Jack, a bachelor had no-one at home, he had called his mother, telling her that he had been working overtime so for her birthday in two weeks, he would have enough for the rent and her present. He lived with her, she struggled with money and he looked after her when she wasn't working. Many of the others within the team were the same. Elderly parents or children that relied on them.

"Still, you shouldn't have."

I shrugged. "I need to eat just as much as you do. Now eat up or I'll tell Ann." That soon made him change his tune. The last thing Ann needed to know was that he wasn't eating. She'd soon tell him it wasn't good for him. I looked at my team, who were grabbing food as they worked. Joining them I grabbed a plate and sat down watching. It felt good to be apart of this team. We looked out for one another on the job and at the station.

"Ma'am." Jack had appeared. "I found some of those files you had asked for. Also, the coroner is ready for you and Sergeant Jeffries."

"Thanks Jack, put the files on my desk and grab something to eat." I stood pulling my jacket on in one swift motion.

"Let's go." I said to Sergeant Jeffries. We headed down to the morgue.

A walk down to the morgue had stretched my aching muscles. Usually there were times I wished I smoked. It certainly would ease the stress, I would feel like Sherlock Holmes, puffing on his pipe while he figured out his latest puzzle, outside the station of course. I hadn't touched a cigarette in years. The walk-in winters fresh air usually woke me up easier and eased the stress. Once we had seen the coroner, that is what I would do. Go for a walk.

Striding through the morgue doors was always an interesting experience. It was dank, dark and the smell of formaldehyde was always overpowering. The air, frosty felt as though we had crossed into Death's domain. It never failed to send a shiver up my spine every time.

The technician was waiting for us beside the coroner and forensics team. This was grave. Usually only one or two of them were waiting for us, but all of them. This was not boding well.

"What do we have Mary?" I asked, although the feeling I had that this was the beginning only intensified. I hoped it sounded strong. I didn't feel strong at that moment.

"Honoria Chapman." Mary, the forensics technician, the boss of the morgue team said. "She used to be Henry Chapman; she was a student. Surgery from two years ago to correct the genitals when she was eighteen. The killer has removed five of her teeth, leaving a laceration on the tongue. We are still figuring the laceration out. There's a bruise down the lower side of the jaw, on the right-hand side, we conclude could be from the size, a fist or a thumb. Neither has been ruled out yet. On the left-hand side of the neck, there is an inch-deep incision, just below the jaw. This runs at four inches in length and runs to immediately below the ear. Below that, is where it gets interesting. Another inch cut has severed the vertebrae in the neck, and all the large vessels in the neck have been severed and is eight inches in length. The cuts all seem to have been made with the same knife, this would be long-bladed in structure, sharp and has been used in the most violent way to cause as much damage as possible."

Jeffries, it seemed close to losing his breakfast. I had to admit I was close to following suit.

"So, where did the blood for all this go?" I asked quietly. "There had to be an awful amount, hitting the major artery."

"I knew you were going to ask that Mags. Well, as you say, the arterial blood would have stained her clothes. But no blood was found on the breast of the body or on any of her clothes. This is unusual. She should be coated." Mary paused. "But it was when we looked at the abdomen that we thought this was a homicide of intent."

"What do you mean?" Jeffries asked. I could hear his voice change in anger. He was against violence to women, in any shape or form. Something I had learned later.

"Well, if you look." We did. "There are more injuries in the lower abdomen."

"Jesus Christ!" Jeffries exclaimed. "The killer butchered her!"

Mary I could see was uneasy at showing us this. Words would not help. So, I looked closer.

"The left side is where there are two or three jagged incisions. Deep and with smaller incisions that go across the top tissues of the abdomen to the right-hand side." Mary's voice was shaking. "It was hard to see whether this was a violent downward jagged motion or not at this stage."

"Could it be that the killer is left-handed?" I asked. Noticing the patterns of the way the incisions were angled.

"Quite possibly."

"What do you mean possibly, is he or isn't he?" Jeffries asked.

"Well, it could be that someone may want you to believe that. It is unclear and I wish I could be clearer." Mary added, she glanced at me. "It was all done with one instrument, this killer is smart or at least pretending to be." The fear was clear in her eyes. "Please Mags, be careful. I have never seen these types of injuries before. It may also have been premediated."

I thanked her, Jeffries seemingly more in shock than I was. We left, my hands beginning to shake. Silence met our walk. Mary's fear ridden eyes was clear. The targets were female or looked like female. It could mean I was at risk of being a target.

Chapter 2

It was exactly as I had feared. It was beginning, again. A copy though as the original would have been dead...unless...no that was anuncommon thing to think. Dead people do not come back to life to kill. Or...would they?

My rational mind argued with my un-rational- the side that believed in ghosts, ghouls and goblins. It wasn't scientific fact that people rose from the dead. So that was not possible.

As we approached the team's area, Jeffries asked. "Mags, you know something don't you?"

"I cannot be sure, but well with my name most people jump to one conclusion. And I am sorry to say that I too jumped to that conclusion." I said quietly. "A copycat Jack the Ripper."

I knew Jeffries would disagree this. And he did. "No way. At least let us find the facts before we jump to that conclusion, and anyone off this team that says different, well I'll put them straight." He looked me dead in the eye before continuing. "Just because you're an Abberline, doesn't mean every case is Jack the Ripper." Before he left to go into our team's area. That was when I needed some air.

I left the building, the cold morning air that had a low sun, mist covering the sun. I did wonder why my ancestor had continued his line. Was it in case of something happening like this? Did he have an opium vision of the future where his line would be needed in the police force again? Well, they all said he was crazy and a drug user. Especially after the death of his first wife.

On that note, I left the chilly and misty air back into the warmth. I would be expected to address the team. I knew Jeffries would already have informed them of the coroner's report. The file evidence would follow once they had completed their full examination. On my entrance, the breakfast station had been cleaned, no evidence of any food remained. That I was glad of. We were ready to begin.

Whiteboards had been stationed for our investigation. Already Jeffries had placed the woman's name in the middle, I could see several the team searching for a recent photograph, searching our records for any criminal activity and any information they could on the victim. I had a good team, not many Detective Inspector's could say the same. They needed very little direction, and when they did need it, they knew my door was open, unless I had a meeting with someone.

"Right Ma'am, files say Henry Chapman was arrested once in a case of an assault on a man. Man was in his early twenties, outside a nightclub in the East End. Files also say that it was because the man called him a ladyboy because he was halfway through his transition to a woman. No other records on Honoria Chapman." That was Amy, she was another member of the team and had also gone through the transition from man to woman. No-one knew except me.

"Thanks Amy, good work. Let's see if we can find that man. When was this?"

Amy checked the records. "About three months ago Ma'am."

"Right, see if we can find the man involved. Perhaps he knew of Honoria's whereabouts before she died. He's a lead at least to start with."

I went over to the whiteboard. Made a link with three month ago. I wrote. Honoria went through transition to become a woman three months ago- was halfway through the transition. I still had a sneaking suspicion this was a copycat, although as Jeffries said, there was no way. Just because my last name was Abberline, did not make this a Jack the Ripper likelihood. If I broached this with my team, all respect that they had for me would be lost. I had to keep this under my belt for now.

"Ma'am, you have a call." Jack said, his hand waving at me. "Says it's urgent."

"Thanks Jack, I will take it in my office, pop it through."

I sat down in my sturdy chair and picked up the phone.

"Hello, Detective Inspector Abberline speaking."

"Oh, My stars! An Abberline in the flesh! I have wanted to tell you that you are all in very real danger."

"What kind of danger?"

"The danger or repeating the past."

"Who are you? Do you know you can be arrested for wasting police time? I suggest you make your point quicker."

I hated my name sometimes, it made people act like fools.

"I am Joseph Barnet; I study history in the East End."

I signed. "A Ripperologist am I right?"

"Not just the Ripper."

I cut him off. "Listen, I know the mistakes of the past and I don't plan on repeating them. I suggest that you don't call this number again unless you have solid evidence or proof. Thank you for your time." I hung up the phone and thumbed my temple. Ripperologists came out of the woodwork every so often, especially when they hear my name. They think that like my ancestor I will allow an investigation to be misled or without justification be a failure. They were half the reason why I hated being who I was. The other half was because of personal reasons. I wasn't good at sharing.

I opened the files that Jack had found, and to my utter distress, the only thing that was found was in 1888. I sighed. Time to see who could be next. Potential witness stories from back then and try and make some form of connection, that way I would be ahead of the game, should another body be discovered. I would make it so that, that would never happen.

I researched long into the day, only stopping to grab a coffee with the team and catch up with what they had found. Which unfortunately wasn't much, although they had managed to contact a friend of the deceased. The friend would be appearing that afternoon, as soon as they had finished work. They had also discovered a partner, who had a history with domestic abuse. They had already spoken with him, he had an alibi, and he seemed generally shocked.

On seeing the friend that afternoon, I could see that they too were shocked and ended the interview on them bawling their eyes out, and an alibi that checked out. I told her to let us know if she can think of anything else and let her go on her way.

We were coming up short. This wasn't good. So, on a note, the team and I went and searched Honoria's flat. What we found there...well it wasn't pretty. In one room, it made Jeffries leave, and I was close to it as a mature woman...well, it would haunt my sleeping hours. The room was filled with several sex contraptions that all of us wanted to know nothing about. The bedroom was messy, and a musty smell filled the place. The landlord had been sending letters about rent etc. there was a pile behind the door, as if she had merely opened the door, pushing the notices, letters etc. to one side in one heap. The only place that was clean, was the kitchen. Gleaming white. That I found odd. Her bathroom was filthy as well. So why was the kitchen clean?

When Amy opened the fridge, we found out why. In her fridge, instead of food we found makeup that needed to be kept cool. No food in the cupboards, which again was unusual. Everything in that kitchen was as bare as the old woman who lived in a shoe. Just minus the children or animals.

In the end we had to return to the station.

No leads.

No witnesses.

No strong case.

What were we going to do?

I sent everyone home for the night at five pm. We had done enough for the day. Before I left, I sat in the team's room, staring at the whiteboard with Honoria's face. I tried to make sense of this. Any of it! Her pictures of her autopsy sat on the whiteboard, so we could see the injuries. I was determined that no one else would end up like her. No-one, or I wasn't an Abberline.

Determined I left the station, hoping that the next day would lead more results. Hopeful.

At least that was what I had told myself, until eight days later.

We had another woman found.

This time, she was found by a neighbour.

"Team, we've got another one!" I called throwing my coat on. We were being admonished in the streets for doing our jobs, thanks to the papers. Tensions ran high in the room, each of us striving to be the ones to end this. Hopefully, although I hated feeling that way, this would help us find the killer, and the papers would stop calling us failures. We would be able to redeem ourselves. But I should know, pride doth come before a fall.

The scene that we arrived on, was far worse than the first murder. And this time, there was a witness. Her body was found in a garden at four forty am on Hanbury Street.

A neighbour had stepped outside for a cigarette and discovered the body. That poor neighbour was in hysterics and Amy was in the process of calming her down. She was after all one of the gentlest in the team. Amy was able to get statement down, that I could depend on her for. It would be as detailed as possible.

I glanced at the area that forensics were working on, this time, even we could see the blood spray up the fence. From where I was, anyway, Mary was working her magic deftly and with precision. We couldn't move the body until she had finished. Then she could take the body and delve deeper. Photographs were being taken of positioning; the press were being kept at bay this time. Thankfully. Right now, all we knew about this woman, was she was a Jane Doe.

When I had seen the body first, I was ashamed to admit I had wanted to throw up. The killer had really enjoyed what he had done to this poor woman. It had been well thought out. It had a pattern to it this time. As though the killer had tried to create a still life painting.

Mary called me over. "Mags, this is bad. Worse than last time." I could tell by her voice that she didn't want to tell me the extent.

"Ok, Mary, just tell us the simple facts. We can wait for the full report later." I said. Trying to offer a smile.

"She has been mutilated." Mary whispered. "Her dress, well it was pulled down over her abdomen. The slash across the throat is deeper and more calculated. He also draped her intestines across her neck like a necklace." Mary had turned white, whiter than the apron she wore. "Her organs are missing some. He knew what he was taking."

"Let us know what's missing Mary." I said, addressing the team. "Right, fan out. See if anyone heard anything, saw anything."

"Right o Ma'am!" They called and with vigour they got to work.

I knew this was the same killer, just more calculated. Was his first a test? Did he feel like he was a winner? Defeating the police, an Abberline, just like last time? Is he gloating? Had he found delight in taking more care with this one?

It made me feel sick. So, I merely surveyed the scene. The backyards that lined Hanbury Street, I found with some difficulty, having to jump and hold onto a fence to see clearly, I cursed my height sometimes. There was no way out unless he was an Olympic vaulter. No-one who wasn't couldn't vault over five-foot-high fences. That was when I looked at the garden. It was overgrown and unkempt. I forced my eyes to scan the ground, urging a piece of evidence to come forward, leaping from the ground. And that's when my heart jumped to my throat. In a heap in the corner was some brown leather.

When we had returned to the office, the team and I processed the statements. We were waiting for the report from Mary. I knew from my research that the organs that would be found missing would be the uterus and the bladder- part of that would be missing. But I waited for Mary to confirm that. The leather had already been tested. The neighbour who had found the body, had already confirmed that had been hers. How it had gotten outside from the airing cupboard in her home, she had no idea. Her husband had confirmed that the neighbour had not gone into the airing cupboard and was knocked out with sleeping tablets for most of the day while he had been at work the following day. We determined after discussing when they had last seen it, that it had been missing for at least a week. That was when the neighbour had placed in the airing cupboard and had been unable to find it since. When they had been asked why they hadn't reported it, the husband had scoffed. "Report a piece of leather missing? That's bonkers and you lot are useless!"

A reliable source, I had discovered was a document on the two murders in 1888. They both in 1888 and now matched up exactly so far. Now it was a waiting game for the report from Mary.

"Ma'am, the reports in!" Jack called.

Jeffries and I jumped up as though we had been shocked and paced down to the morgue. Now we would discover how this poor woman had died and her name.

The details were horrific.

"The killer had placed her left arm over her left breast. Her legs were drawn up to make her feet be flat on the ground. The knees therefore were pointing outwards. Her face is abnormally swollen, it was leaned to the right. On her right eyelid, there is a bruise and it matches to one on her temple. He made it so the tongue is protruding between the front teeth, but so much that you can see it through the lips. The tongue is also swollen." Mary paused. Her hands were shaking slightly as well. "She has also been horribly mutilated. Her limbs are unmarked, so no defence wounds. The throat has been deeply cut, to the point where she has nearly been beheaded. The blood on the wall, I compared the photographs to the scene. The blood spray is fourteen inches from where her head is. So, we can confirm the blood is her arterial spray. Again, the same instrument was used on the throat and abdomen."

Mary had to pause again, and she swallowed hard. "There are bruises on her chest, such as the size of a large thumb."

"If you need to have a break Mary-"Jeffries began.

"No, you need to know the details so you can catch this bastard." Mary said almost savagely.

She took a deep breath. And then continued. "Her abdomen cavity was opened completely and what we found in there, well it made even my toughest assistant sick. Her intestines had been completely severed, hence the necklace. Her uterus, vagina and all other reproductive organs have been removed, and we didn't find them at the scene. So, it is likely he has them, as a trophy of some kind. Two thirds of her bladder are also missing. He has used long blades on both victims. But because of this body I can determine they are six to eight inches in length. I want to say a bayonet, or a sword's bayonet. But this could also be a knife like this." She held up a mortuary knife. That was long and looked deadly. "She has also been dead for two hours. There was a handkerchief tied around her neck, we've sent that for testing as well."

Hearing Mary's words I was stunned. He was becoming more brutal. This victim had been brutally murdered. Destroyed. Mary was affected, pale and white knuckles. Jeffries too was affected. He had gone as white as the corpse in front of us. I took a deep breath. "So, look for mortuary knives, in five to eight inches in length?"

Mary nodded. "If you can find one and it matches then you could find the killer, before he kills again. Find that knife and you find the murderer."

"Mary, I hate to ask, but do you think women are the key targets or at least people who act like women?" I shuddered.

"I believe so." Her reply was so quiet I didn't hear it at first. "If I hadn't have seen the first murder then I would have said transgender women would be, but this is a woman who was born a woman. So, it could be any female, like you or I."

Mary's words circled in my thoughts, like the vultures that they were. One was more daunting as the last. I could be a target. I looked up and Amy crossed into my vision. Or Amy?

Our killer was also sporadic. He jumped from transgender to female, was he just recreating or was there an underlying hatred there? I still was unsure that I should tell the team about my theory. But I knew that someone would reach the same conclusion I had. All of them were logical, researching, and they came to answers rather quickly.

As I thought this, Max came running towards me, out of breath and as if he had just run a marathon. Max was a middle-aged man who liked alcohol a little too much when off duty. But as a worker he was unfathomable.

"Mags! It could be a copycat!" He breathed at once. "I've done the research; all the injuries match up with a Jack the Ripper cop cat!"

"Max, deep breath, I can't understand." I said gently. Although I heard what he had said.

He took a deep breath and repeated.

Jeffries immediately jumped on it. "No way. That's not what we have here."

"The injuries match." Max said defiantly. "Sarg. Honest. I typed in copycat murders and the injuries match. They are the same."

"No." Jeffries scoffed. "Any injuries could match; it doesn't mean we have a copycat."

"I have deduced the same thing Max." I said, Jeffries merely stared. "It's worth checking for others as well. We'll have a couple of people working on potential copycats the rest of us, get out there and see if we can find who this poor woman was." I said.

"Right away Ma'am!" They chorused.

"On the plus side Mags, we arrested someone." Jeffries said. "I am going to go and interrogate him now. He had a knife on him, so we thought we would chase it up. It is a similar size knife we are looking for." I could tell he wanted to steer away from the conspiracy that was a Jack the Ripper copycat.

"Great work. Let's see if he's connected. I will let you and Amy take this one." Amy perked up at this. I was hoping for her to gain more experience in interrogations. "We can see how he reacts to having her in the room also." I sighed. "Jeffries, I am sorry."

"What for Mags?" Then he smiled. "Your name may be an Abberline, but you are doing more than what your ancestor did. Our team respects you. Let's catch him together!"

I smiled. "Let's catch him." Jeffries and Amy left to go and interrogate the man we had in the cell. I went to the room with the two-sided glass mirror. I could watch his reactions from there. He was an ordinary man, that was for sure.

"So why did you have the knife on you?" Amy asked. They had been in there for thirty minutes. And he showed no signs of anger. Until Amy spoke. His face changed; the look of disgust was clear. He refused to answer her questions and waited for Jeffries to repeat. He then began to call her a multiple of things, things that I was disgusted to hear. Jeffries brought Amy out and took Max back in with him. Amy looked close to tears.

"Don't listen to what he says Amy." I said. "Men like that are despicable. There is a reason why many of them end up behind bars. Your safe here."

"Thanks Mags." She said quietly. "Do you think it's him?"

"Who knows Amy, who knows." I said. Not quite believing we would have caught the killer this quickly.

It turned out that we hadn't as he had, had an alibi that checked out at the time of each of the murders and the knife we confiscated was the wrong knife. We had to let the suspect go. As he left, he called me and Amy some nasty things, which he was warned if he carried on, he would end back in the cells. He quietened down and left, only throwing some dirty looks at us as he left.

We were back to square one.

Nothing. No leads, no suspects.

We still had no ID on the Jane Doe either. She wasn't in the records, or in the missing persons. So, the team had to walk around with the mortuary photo, her body draped to prevent showing off the injuries.

Until we had a hit. Someone said they recognised her. Her name was Barbara Nicholls. A woman of thirty, a huge contrast to her predecessor. She had been a teacher. They hadn't reported her missing, because the following two days she had called in with a stomach virus. And it turned out that she lived near Durward Street. Where the first murder occurred. There was a connection there. That I was sure of. Her boss seemed stricken to have to come and identify her, but he was sure it was her. He even showed the team a recent photograph. Barbara Nicholls, how did she link? A teacher and a transgender student, did we have a murderer at schools? That was worrying. We had to do everything in our power to stop more ending up like these two.

We had to catch this guy, we just had to!

Chapter 3

Four weeks later...

We had been chastised, ridiculed by the public and our fellow police officers. My team and I, we were brow beaten, defeated, failures. We had failed. The killer was still roaming free. It was as if he was a ghost.

Many of my team now believed that my theory was true and was using the archives of the 1888 Jack the Ripper case as a basis, though we would never admit that to the public. Subdued and banter less in the team room, we worked in near enough silence. We had more tension than ever, more of a reason, because we all believed he would strike again.

We kept researching where the old streets were for the last three murders, and we patrolled those areas every night. Myself more than others, to Jeffries's dismay.

He feared that I would be next, one of the victim's but my argument was that if I didn't do my bit then the killer would just be another killer to taunt my family. That would never happen again to an Abberline.

Then we got a lead.

We hunted the lead down until we discovered...it was a fake! A plant sent in by the local paper. Telling us that we had bungled both murders now. The leather apron it turned out was a fake clue, someone had planted that, that night, before the neighbour found the deceased girl, wiping her blood-which explained the smear on the fence, onto the apron before dropping it.

In the streets were heckled, spat at and taunted. I feared more for my team than me. They were not used to such things; I had been dealing with this for the whole of my thirty-five years. Every word aimed at us were stones, I felt them more keenly since I was in charge. I tried to take the brunt of every word, to save them from the embarrassment. They all had lives. I did not. They used to laugh and say I was married to my job, and I used to be able to laugh that off. Not now. Not when the so-called marriage was almost like being taken through a divorce, a rough and messy one.

Whenever I looked in the mirror, I had aged. Daily. The same could be said for my team. Whereas I was the one not sleeping, not really eating, I encouraged them all to. I would pretend for the sake of them. I was a master at pretending everything was fine, when it was a disaster.

This continued until the thirtieth of September.

I had been pacing at home, it wasn't my shift to walk the streets and part of me wanted to march out there and go on shift anyway. I had been forced home. Jeffries had almost ordered me to, when he had seen how pale I had gotten and the deeper blue bruised bags under my eyes. But I couldn't rest. Not until we had caught this killer. I was looking deep into what Sherlock Holmes would have called my mind palace. A picture on my living room wall, that held the 1888 murders on them. With a date and a name of the new victims. A question mark for each of the following that we wanted to stop happening. But nothing was becoming clear! That was when I took the hidden box of cigarettes, from the place on my mantelpiece. I had to have one! It may have eased the stress and anger I had felt.

Just as I had pulled a lighter from my pocket, my phone rang. I looked at the cigarette and lit it before answering the phone.

"Nothing yet Mags." It was just Jeffries checking in.

"Thanks Bill." I sighed and took a deep draught on the cigarette as we hung up. The great detective would have found me lacking. Nothing more than a shoddy policeman, making shoddy mistakes. Well a woman in this case making shoddy mistakes. I sat down heavily on my sofa, the cigarette my only companion that night. I had a feeling it would be tonight. After all it was the thirtieth of September, the date that the double murder would occur. I wanted to hope against hope that my team prevented this. We couldn't take much more disappointment.

Looking for inspiration, I looked at the antique grandfather clock I had received from my own late grandfather, the only member of the family to care how well I progressed in life. I had been closer to him than my parents and siblings. I was the only daughter in the family. That didn't amount to much. My brothers always fought and strived for being the alpha of the family, my father encouraging them. My mother, well she was very much a trophy woman. She kept house and became a mindless drone who did what my father wanted her to do. It wasn't much effort to persuade her. When I brought up that I wanted to join the police force, rather than get married and become a lawyer and a mother, that had caused roars of laughter all around. The only one who stood up for me was my grandfather. He had said, 'it was a bout time that an Abberline re-joined the police force.' And he encouraged me when my family told me I would never make it, never amount to much. That I would be stuck on a desk job for much of my career. Grandfather told me to ignore the simple-minded fools. He believed in me. And he did until his dying day, when my family disowned me. The clock was all I received from them, telling me that if grandfather wanted me to have it then I would, as none of them wanted it.

I remembered back when I had graduated from the academy. My only supporter, telling me I did the Abberline name proud. Told me he was proud, watching me receive my medal. Watched me become a Detective Inspector before his heart gave out on him. He had a goofy grin on his face when I received my badge. I wanted to remember him like that, not connected to tubes to keep him alive until we all said goodbye. Before he passed, he told me in between breaths where he hissed, and wheezed, that when things looked tough all I had to do was to look at it at another angle. That had been passed down from his father and his father's father. Passing down my only inheritance. When I had been thrown from the hospital after he left me, disowned and alone in the world I remembered that. I was the black sheep, the disgrace, the one no-one talked about in the family tree and at reunions. I didn't care. My team was my family. That was why I was so determined to help them, to let this all be over with.

I had lit another cigarette and stood outside my apartment on my balcony, watching cars and people go past. Was this how my ancestor had felt? Being passed by? Life had passed him by.Having had his career dashed with the uncatchable killer? Having the Abberline name truly dashed into the mud? Is this what my true family legacy was? To lose faith in ourselves when we hit complete the lowest of the low?

Before I had known it, I heard my doorbell ringing. Stumping out the cigarette, closing the balcony doors I answered it, my stomach churning. It would not be good news. That I was doubly sure of.

"Mags, there's been another murder!" It was Bill Jeffries, my sergeant.

I grabbed my coat, hat and keys, locked the door and threw on my coat and hat before following. My worst fear had come true.

We arrived on the scene no later than ten minutes. Thirtieth September. I prewarned my team, who had gathered there, preventing the public from having access. That it may not be the only murder tonight and to keep an eye out for anyone suspicious.

I walked with Jeffries over to the corpse. "Forensics are on their way." Jeffries said. So, I surveyed the scene, not wanting to disturb the scene. Right away, I could see why this was different. Why Ripperologists believed that Liz Stride was not one of the Ripper's victims. However, our copycat believed different it seemed. Henriques Street. Where Berner Street existed in 1888. She had been hidden in what used to be

Dutfield's Yard, a narrow passageway. There, just like back in 1888 was a witness. He was being soothed by my amazing team. I looked at my watch. It was a little after one. I had asked Jack and Max to look at the area where Catherine Eddowes had been discovered. Especially around the Mitre Square area. Just in case. If they didn't an hour from now, we would have another brutally murdered woman.

Looking at that corpse, I already would know what the coroner and forensics would see. A still cooling body. Her throat slit like the others. Blood drained. No blood splatter from an arterial spray. The team said when they had found her, a black scarf was wrapped around her neck pulled tight in a from the knot, which still sat there. They had not touched the body. As I stood there, I overheard the distressed shout of the witness. "She was still warm when I found her!" That meant the killer had not long fled the scene. Just looking I could see she had not been mutilated. So that meant our witness had to have seen the killer! He had to have disturbed him. A dark flower was pinned to her dress-one that had been clearly for clubbing, it was unclear if the flower was pinned post-mortem or premortem. It gave a huge indication of her age. My watch read, one fifteen. So, in an hour we would either get our killer or see another body.

I wanted to believe it would be the former, rather than the latter. But it would be more that our killer would have already found his victim and would be in the process of killing her. He would destroy her.

Instead of hanging around the area waiting for forensics, I made my way to Mitre Square much to Jeffries despair. So of course, he had to follow me.

"What is the purpose?" He asked. "Your going to get yourself killed!"

"Rather me than some innocent!" I yelled as I ran towards the square. I panted looking around me. There was no-one around. No! No! I wanted to scream in frustration. I couldn't have been too late! I glanced at my watch. One forty-five. That meant he was here! Surely!I ran around in desperation, looking left and right. That's when I saw it. A shadow. A darker than the shadows of hell figure. I gave chase.

It ran left and right before I was right on top of it...it vanished. I crashed to the floor in disbelief. "Ouch!" I rubbed my head, feeling blood but right then not caring. "No way! No freaking way!" I screamed. "Some stupid ghost is killing people, no way in living hell!"

"Mags?! Mags! Are you okay?!" Jeffries had arrived.

"I nearly had him Bill, he vanished!"

"What Mags, people don't just disappear."

"This one did. I lunged for him and he disappeared, hence why I am on the floor." I sighed. "Let me guess, there's a body?"

"How did you know?" Jeffries said sarcastically.

"Funny guess." I responded just as sarcastically. Jeffries extended a hand to help me up. My knees buckled. Jeffries caught me before I fell.

"Thanks Bill."

"No worries Mags, I've got you." Together we slowly made our way back to the square. What would meet us there, that was what I was afraid of.

Chapter 4

It was exactly as I had feared. As I was being fussed over, someone wanted to check me for concussion, at Jeffries behest. A body that was horribly disfigured. I realised my role in this was at that moment the P.C that found the body in 1888. Rather than the Inspector Abberline.

It was a place at the right moment time. And I had played my part well. I just had felt him literally pass through my hands. I couldn't believe it. I had come so close to catching this monster.

I was told to go home, but instead I went to the station-to my office. I would await the results from the coroner there. My team soon filed into the room not long after.

They seemed surprised to see me, but instead of telling me to leave, they brought me a kebab from the pizza shop. I thanked them and ate. I knew I needed to with the strong painkillers I had been given.

"For what it's worth Mags Ma'am." I heard Max, Jack and Amy say as a chorus. "We believe that you are telling the truth about nearly catching him."

"Thanks, you three, you're the only ones." I said throwing my finished kebab into the bin. "Everyone else thinks I'm hallucinating or concussed. But I know what I saw."

They nodded.

"Has forensics returned?" I asked.

"Yes, they are doing the autopsy now." Max replied.

I glanced through to the whiteboards with our victims. There was something bugging me about them and this new one.

"Find a connection between our four victims. Start with the first three, then when we know this one's name find the connection between those three and her." I said pointing. "There has to be a connection. Just we aren't seeing it yet."

I grabbed a white board and started writing things down feverishly. "Ok what do we know about Honoria?"

"She was a student and went to the same place that the second victim went." Max responded. I was glad to see the three taking notes.

"Good. So, Barbara Nicholls, what do we know that link these two together?"

"School." Jack said. "So, we look into school records!"

"Yes! See if we can find out who this third victim is! Take a photograph and investigate the school in the morning." I drew a line between Honoria, Barbara and Jane Doe. Underneath I wrote school is the same. Our one and only link. That had to be it!

When Jeffries came in an hour later, from the square, he saw us all huddled in the room with coffees and piles of information regarding the school. Mainly what we had gathered from the website until the school opened at seven am.

"What on Earth is going on?" He asked sceptically.

"Sarg. We found a link or rather Mags did." Max said beaming. "It's the school."

"The school?" He questioned, looking at me. I must have looked the most unprofessional he had ever seen me.

"The school, Honoria was a student, Barbara was a teacher, if we can find the third and fourth victim in here that's our link!" I smiled, despite how weary I really felt. "That means the killer is either at the school or is from that area!"

Jeffries smiled too. Finally!We were getting somewhere! He joined us in the huddle though we had to move onto chairs soon, as most of us were struggling with seeing in a huge pile. So, like the investigators that we were, as a team we took a few each at a time.

That was until...

"Mags! I found her victim number three!" Jack scampered over to where I was working.

"Great job Jack, who is she?!" I said pulling the whiteboard, ready for note taking.

"Marjorie Blyth. Nineteen. She has a party lifestyle. No family but is also on file for a small theft when she was fourteen." Jack continued. "It was a convenience store theft, and she paid the money in when she was caught."

I wrote exactly what Jack said onto the board. We had our link!

"Right get a list of all the teachers, students and other staff that work at that school. I need two of you to go in when the school opens in." I paused and glanced at my watch. "thirty minutes." I looked at my team, then realised. "If you have a change of clothes, get changed if not please pop home on your way, shower, change and get something to eat. This is our only solid lead, and while the forensics are busy with our fourth victim, I will be looking at the area around the school." I said.

To my surprise, my team looked at each other and then respectfully saluted. "Aye, aye Ma'am." Then broke into laughter.

"Alright, you lot off you go." I laughed. "Make sure you eat something!" I called after them.

"Same goes for you Mags!" I heard Jeffries call. I knew what I would do, I would wash and change in the police bathroom, after putting the room in a lockdown of course. This meant locking the doors to our team's room, a mistake that we hadn't thought about before, but I wasn't going to let our one and only link leak. I had a sinking suspicion that we were being hindered. But by who or what I wasn't sure.

I did just that. On my way to the bathroom I locked the doors behind me. I changed and washed quickly before leaving the station. I knew I needed breakfast, and I grabbed a takeaway bacon roll from a local food truck, and a coffee. On my return to the station, I saw Jeffries waiting outside.

"Sorry Bill, I wanted to grab something to eat. Here's the key." I placed my bacon roll on top of my coffee and grabbed the keys from my coat pocket.

"No problem Mags." He looked refreshed too. He unlocked the door and we went in. Everything was just as we left it.

"Have you heard from the others?" I asked as I went into my office. Jeffries following. My coffee and roll I placed to one side of my desk.

"Yup, Jack and Max are at the school. Amy has gone home for a quick nap, as she looked dead on her feet. I made sure she was in the house and door was locked before I left." He looked a little concerned.

"What's wrong?" I asked.

"There were quite a few people hanging around her flat. I was worried that our Amy was next. So, I urged her to ring us when she woke up, that way Jack and Max could stop by and pick her up, I could be wrong, but my gut is never wrong."

"Good call." I said. He looked a bit relieved. "I am worried about you too Mags."

"Me why?" I bit into my bacon roll. I almost moaned in delight.

"Not that I don't think you can take care of yourself. Not at all. But…"He trailed off.

"Thanks for caring Bill, it means the world to me. But I am fine."

"I know Mags, but if this killer's target is women then…well you and Amy are targets." Jeffries said. I could see how worried he was. I smiled. "If you want, when I leave mine, I will ask you all to meet me and ask Amy to do the same." He gave a big sigh of relief.

"That would be a good idea Mags, thanks for listening." He smiled. I took the chance to really look at him, my sergeant. He was a stout, middle-aged man, with greying hair and twinkling grey eyes. Happily married and always dressed well, never let his fear usually dictate his actions. I was thankful I had a kind of father figure.

"Bill, anytime you know that. I value your opinion. I would rather we work together than go off and put myself in danger." I binned my paper off my bacon roll and took a deep swig of my coffee. Then I dug into my bag and grabbed the packet of cigarettes.

"I didn't know you were smoking again?" Jeffries asked.

"Stress got to me." I responded. I patted my pocket for a lighter and when I found one, I stood. "Your welcome to come with me outside but can you lock up?" I asked.

"Sure." Jeffries said, standing with me. I could see I brought out his protective instincts. And it brought a smile to my face, Jeffries cared about women in an old- fashioned view, in times like this I respected it.

As we stood out in the misty air, I smoked, imagining that the cigarette was an escape. Jeffries beside me, in companionable silence. My Watson to my Sherlock.

I stumped out the cigarette. "Thanks Bill, I needed the air and a smoke."

"No problem. I reckon we might have our forensics results now."

"Here's hoping." I looked out to the morning sky as it lightened. It appears as a symbol of hope. The sun beginning to shine again, after a long time of darkness. I closed my eyes as the sun hit my face.

"Now that's nice to see." Jeffries said beside me. "Hope."

"I agree." I opened my eyes and waved him inside. "Despite hope we have results to get."

"Aye, aye." Jeffries laughed.

So, we made our way from the brilliant white and warm light into the dark and dank that was the police morgue.

On our arrival, we saw Mary standing outside. Tear tracks lined her cheeks, and I could see the terror and horror in her eyes.

"Mary." I breathed. "It's ok, we are a step closer to catching this killer. I swear it."

"Please do, because this was his worst yet. I had multiple assistants throw up during the autopsy, outside of course." Mary wiped her cheeks. "I feel humiliation for the poor girl."

"Do we know who she is?" I asked.

"Gloria Edwards." Mary huffed. It was a huff that this poor woman had suffered at the hands of this killer. "She was twenty -five. Another teacher."

"So, we were right. The killer is targeting a school or an area." I glanced a Jeffries. He looked green.

"Seems so." Mary replied. I patted her shoulder.

"Shall I take the report, rather than have you tell us?"

"No. It's ok, let's go in and I can tell you how horribly she died."

We followed Mary inside where Gloria's body lay.

"So, when I arrived at the scene, beside seeing Mags here being tended to, I saw that Gloria was on her back, her head was turned to her left shoulder. This is quite unusual, howeverwhen I saw the arms I understood why. It was as if she had fallen like that and the killer had left her there while he continued. Both palms upwards, the fingers slightly bent. A thimble was lying off the finger on the right side. The clothes drawn up above the abdomen. The thighs were naked. Left leg extended in a line with the body. The abdomen was exposed. Right leg bent at the thigh and knee.

There was a hat at the back of the head and a great disfigurement of the face. The throat cut. Across below the throat was a handkerchief."

"Similar to Barbara Nicholls." I breathed. "Another calling card?"

"Potentially. Maybe he's marking them as different to the others." Mary said, it worried her and made her fear more apparent. She continued. "Her intestines, they were drawn out to a large extent and placed over the right shoulder—they were smeared over with some faecal matter. A piece of about two feet was quite detached from the body and placed between the body and the left arm, apparently by design. The lobe and auricle of the right ear were cut obliquely through. There was a quantity of clotted blood on the pavement on the left side of the neck round the shoulder and upper part of the arm, and fluid blood-coloured serum which had flowed under the neck to the right shoulder, the pavement sloping in that direction." Mary paused again. We let her, clearly what was coming was worse.

"But it was when we got her back here that we saw the extremity that the killer had gone to."

"She was warm to the touch when I felt her skin in a glove." Jeffries said. "So, does that mean he hadn't long finished?"

"Yes, it had been maybe about a half an hour at most."

"So, I disturbed him from really completing then." I added.

"Seems that way."

"It was when we started washing away blood, that we saw the extent. There were bruises on her hand, quite was red and fresh. Older ones on her shins, as if she had walked into something. She died by haemorrhage from her artery in the carotid region. Thus, death was quick for this one. So, the mutilations occurred after she had died. The murderer would not have had a speck of blood on him."

"So, finding bloody clothes is out of the question." Jeffries said sighing.

"Nope, all the blood would have been on her and at the scene." Mary said, her hands shaking.

"Continue Mary." I said softly. I was disturbed, I was trying to hide it.

"Cuts were made from the right. She's missing her left kidney. As we washed her face, it's clear the killer has tried to hide her identity, cutting and slicing her eyelids, the tip of her nose and across her cheeks, part of her ear had been cut off as well. It doesn't look like he knows anatomy though, he hasn't got the skills of someone who knows animals or the anatomy of people either. So, the killer is acting on a whim or off something that has happened before." Mary trailed off.

"I agree Mary, we feel it's a Ripper copycat." I said plainly. She had to see that as well. She sighed in relief.

"I thought so too. I didn't want to mention, since your ancestor had to witness this in 1888, you are an Abberline and all."

"Thanks for being considerate Mary." I said patting her shoulder. "This is not about me being an Abberline, this is about stopping him before he kills one final time, if he is a copycat. But we have a lead and we are following these up as we speak."

"If that is true, then the final murder would be his worst and most despicable yet." Mary raised her hands to her mouth.

I nodded. "Which is why we are going to stop him. He wont complete it. Not while I still anyway."

"I believe that." Mary said.

"So, do I Mags." Jeffries said. We were a trio of support. We believed in each other and we would stop this monster.

We returned from the morgue, energetic to find this monster, and saw Jack, Max and Amy waiting for us.

"Glad your back." We opened the door with vigour and carried on.

A few days later, we were in the room, working overtime when a courier brought a package to my desk.

"Ma'am this was posted for you." The courier said, a small smile on his face. "The man at the front desk told me to bring through to you."

"Thank you?" I asked, looking up into his brown eyes.

"Oliver Ma'am."

"Oliver, thank you. You can go now." I smiled. He was doing his job well it seemed. I looked at the package. Then screamed.

My team had run straight in, removing me from my own office. The package had been leaking an oozing red liquid, and I knew it was blood. Forensics had been called straight away. And there had been a note.

Ms. Abberline,

Ma'am,

I send you half the kidney I took from one woman, preserved it for you. The other piece I fried and ate, it was very nice. I may send you the bloody knife that took it out if you wait a little longer.

Catch me if you can!

Jack the Ripper

From Hell.

The note had been typed, as we could recognise handwriting these days. And the note was almost directly the same as the From Hell letter the police in 1888 received from George Lusk. The hunt had been on for the courier Oliver, but he had vanished. The courier company had no idea who he was. And all I can remember was those brown eyes. Those eyes that now I thought about, was deep and emotionless. The killer now had their final target it seemed. I was a target, no matter what anyone else on the team thought.

It seemed I had multiple roles in this investigation. The Inspector, the Police Constable and now, it seemed Mary Jane Kelly. Jeffries refused to let me go anywhere without him or another male on our team. It seemed a little extreme to me, but it also allowed me to know about Jack, he was also a smoker, so he accompanied me on my fresh air breaks. Max, it turned out lived near to where I did, so he always picked me up from work and took me home, brought me from home and to work.

Amy was distraught. She had to go on leave. We were down a person, and I worried about her being home by herself. Mary Jane Kelly had been, before the murderer struck, and I didn't want her to be the next victim, we were being watched. This carried on for over a month.

The killer was waiting. We were too. More of us spent time patrolling streets, hoping for a glimpse of him. But to no avail. He was being as elusive as he was back in 1888.

Desperate times called for desperate measures.

I called the Ripperologist back.

"Joseph Barnett?" I asked as the phone picked up.

"Speaking."

"Detective Inspector Abberline."

Line went dead silent.

"I wanted to apologise for before, I didn't realise that these were murders associated with Jack the Ripper and a copycat." I continued.

The line continued to be silent.

"Are you still there?" I asked. I was sure that he had hung up.

"Yes." Came over the phone. "Why now?"

"I wanted to apologise and bring you in as an advisor." I said. I wasn't sure that he would help.

"I repeat, why now? Surely your aware of a fifth and final murder?" He asked. "Why would you need my help now?"

"We have a lead; I am not at liberty to discuss over the phone. But we want your help." I simply stated.

He paused before speaking. "I will be by this afternoon." And hung up.

I listened to the dial tone for a little while.

Then replaced the phone onto the hand-held machine. He would come, he wouldn't come. Either way at least then we would have a potential person of interest. He was being brought in because he had knowledge that until now, we weren't sure who the killer could be.

But we researched Joseph Barnett. Turns out he was harmless, but if bringing him in helped to show who the police leak was, then we could capture the killer. We had a vague idea who the leak was, though we couldn't be sure. So, Jeffries and I would be the only ones who knew the true purpose of inviting Barnett to the station. He would come straight into an interview room, where we would only allow myself and Jeffries into this, locking the door, and making sure no-one could hear in the room opposite.

Jeffries and I had opposing views on the leak. Someone was leaking information to the press. That had to be curbed before we could chase the suspect. We found this out, as the note appeared in the paper the following day after I received it. No-one apart from those in the team and the person at the front desk knew I had a package. So, it narrowed down to a potential six or seven people in total, including myself.

"Ma'am a Joseph Barnett is here to see you." The front desk rang in.

"Thanks Eli. Jeffries and I will be there shortly." I hung up waved at Jeffries and we walked out of the room, the team carried on. Our eyes were open to see anyone who might freeze or look up as we walked past. No-one did.

When we approached the front desk, a young man who looked to be in his later middle ages, dark brunette hair and green eyes that seemed to be concerned for his welfare. He held out a hand and Jeffries and I shook it.

"Joseph Barnett." He said. "I suspect one of you is Detective Inspector Abberline?"

"That would be me." I said, gesturing up the stairs. "Shall we?"

"Am I in trouble?" Barnett asked.

"No, but we are not at liberty to discuss in public." Jeffries spoke before I could.

"Alright." The fear in Barnett's eyes increased. We didn't speak again until we reached the room. I locked the door as I entered. Making sure no-one had gone into the room, by locking the adjoining doors, as we had walked up.

"We apologise for the secrecy. We feel there is someone within the police station who is leaking information to the press. Information that follows is at the most secrecy. We have a lead, this being a school." Jeffries said and I nodded.

"And why are you telling me this?" Barnett asked.

"We don't think you have anything to do with this case, apart from being aware of the murders." I added. "We thought bringing you here, would allow for anybody who had a chance to see you, report that to the press that we are bringing in a potential suspect" I quoted the suspect. "in for questioning."

"I see, that would then be leaked, and you could have an idea who the leak is." Barnett deduced.

"Exactly, our only regret is not bringing you in earlier, we have prevented some of the murders." I sighed. "That was a mistake."

He looked from me to Jeffries. "So, I gather that I am here for another reason?"

He had hit the nail on the head. "Indeed. We wanted to discuss with you, the lead we have is a school. The school has had three students and two teachers murdered. Has anyone contacted you that they are doing research for a paper, coursework or other methods?"

Barnett thought. "There was someone about twelve months ago. But it was a genuine question unrelated to the murders themselves."

"What did they ask?" I leant forward. Could that be our killer?

"About whether there were actually five murders or in my opinion were there more, I believe they asked." He paused. "It was a male. Couldn't tell you the age. He didn't like my reply however."

"What was your reply?" Jeffries asked.

"I told him unless this was for a paper and I was to be cited I couldn't help." Barnett replied. "I don't discuss my theories unless it is for work and work only."

Jeffries and I leaned back. At least Barnett hadn't started this by feeding information.

"Did I do the right thing?" He asked a twinge of fear in his voice. "Because if I started this by refusing..."

"No Mr Barnett, we feel that if you had you would have fed the killer information. You have not done so. However, it is unfortunate that this potential killer has taken the path of anger and revenge. We feel that he may use you as a scapegoat." I added.

"A scapegoat?" Barnett nearly jumped from the chair. "But I did nothing!"

"We know. And we are fully prepared to take all your statements about your phone call. That way we have it on file, before the press get a hold of it." Jeffries said soothingly.

Barnett visibly calmed. "Anything that I can do, I shall." He replied.

"Let's get started." I said with a smile.

An hour later and the information was put on file.

Barnett thanked us before he left, tipping his hat at me. "Anything else I can do, please ask," He had added. I nodded, knowing we would be calling him soon. He was to be a role play around the area as a boyfriend of mine or Amy's once we had narrowed down who the target was.

It had to be one of us, as it seemed that the killer had already had a plan in motion. We had plainclothes policemen walking around areas in Whitechapel where Mary Jane Kelly would have lived, and other office areas, warehouses that were near that area.

Mary Jane Kelly lived in thirteen Miller's Court, that didn't exist today. White's Row Car Park did. And this was on the site where Mary Jane Kelly breathed her last. Barnett would also be walking around this area. He had already agreed to go on a Ripper Tour early in the year, that was his final stop on the tour. We all had agreed he would carry on as normal. If he was contacted again, he would inform us with a key word.

Chapter 5

The killer had become silent. He wouldn't strike until November. So, we had a month to prepare. It didn't mean that we let our guards down.

Our leak, the front desk boy had been sacked, and sent to work in the files archives once this had come to its final head, a murder or a suspect in a cell. A punishment that involved being stripped of his badge and gun.

He was not very happy, and he had disagreed with having a woman Detective Inspector.

Mary Jane Kelly, or who she would be today, would either be saved on the ninth of November or murdered. We had an idea that she would either be around the same age or if we were also correct, then it would either be me, Amy or an unknown woman. So, we hunted. And we made it look as though we were on the trail of multiple suspects. But our real target was being watched, he didn't know he was being watched it was not made clear.

We had been tipped off by Barnett. He had been contacted again, this time he confirmed the name we had. Having asked the man his name, the man was unaware that he was being tailed. He was very cocky, assure that he would be successful. The suspect was in fact someone who lived near the school. And he had a deep hatred for women.

He had been tailed by men. Amy and I would work at the desk, going out together to smoke. Seemingly to allow the boys to work.

I had caught the suspect out of the corner of my eye one day, walking past the station when we had been outside. He had glanced at us as he walked past, then carried on without a backwards glance.

Amy and I were a target. That much was clear.

Barnett called me on the fourth of November.

"Detective Inspector Abberline."

"Abberline-"

"Call me Mags Barnett." I said. "It's easier."

"Mags, he has posted something on the Ripper tour I am going on in five days. He asked how long the tour will take as he is interested in where Miller's Court used to be."

"Thanks Barnett."

He paused before asking. "Mags, please join me on the tour. I couldn't fathom if something happened to you. You said Amy is fine, allow us to protect you."

"That's very kind Barnett. But if I were to appear, it would be clear on that we had caught up to him. And it would blow the operation. No, I must be home alone. That is the plan."

"Mags, allow someone to be hidden nearby then."

"Someone will be." I responded. "I live not that far from White's as it is. You will be around the corner."

He went silent for some time. "Then I shall head to your address and hide."

I agreed. "Jeffries will be joining you in the tour. He has already stated this, so you won't be alone."

I hated being used for bait. But in this case, it had to be done. I refused to let Amy be the bait.

Soon, too soon, it was time to put my potential final moments on this earth into motion. I pretended that I had lost my flat key, instead dropping it into Bill's bin, where he grabbed it before the bins were emptied.

I made it clear that I would not need to be walked home. I walked home by myself. It almost gave Jeffries and Barnett a heart attack, but it was necessary. The killer had to see me alone for this to work. And see me alone he did. I smoked out on my balcony and watched him lurking below it, finding which one was my room. I had decided on the ninth of November to leave my door unlocked. Mary Kelly would be impressed. I knew that the killer would not be able to resist.

Jeffriesand Barnett continued to argue with me about risking my life. Jeffries concern was fatherly and a friend. Barnett, I wasn't too sure why he was arguing, considering I didn't know him too well. That made me a touch suspicious, was he working with the killer? But then I shoved that thought aside. Barnett was just showing human concern.

The night of eighth of November rolled around, and I was a bundle of nerves. I had hidden my gun beneath my pillow of my bed, having pretended to go to bed not early, as it was found that Mary Kelly was killed at four thirty am, the killer will want to make sure that this one will fit with that. I would make sure that he and my fellow capturers will see me at one am on my balcony. I would have a cigarette. After this was over, I vowed I would finish smoking for good.

And there I was, at one am. A cigarette in one hand, leaning on the balcony looking up at the stars, seeing the murderer out of the corner of my eye, and on the other side, seeing Barnett and Jeffries. Phase one was already in motion. Phase two would begin as soon as I entered my flat. I didn't want to enter my flat. I didn't want to leave my door open. I didn't want to be killed. To me it didn't make much sense why an Abberline was being targeted. Maybe this killer wanted to show the Ripper in hell he ended an Abberline on the police force. Show that they all are useless. And that his was a woman, would he be welcomed with open arms? I lit one last cigarette and watched the stars. I was petrified.

Once I had smoked the cigarette to death I sighed and stumped it out, leaving the balcony and heading to bed. I hated this. He could either climb up to my balcony or he would come up the stairs through my unlocked door. I lay on the bed, pretending to be asleep when I heard a light thud of the front door closing softly.

Phase three.

My hand under the pillow closed over my gun.

I waited for him to come into the bedroom.

It felt like years was passing and then I remembered, he would want to take his time. Complete this mutilation with plenty, he had plenty of time.

I controlled my breathing, as if I was in a deep slumber. I was good at this acting. I had deliberately placed my most revealing night dress that I owned on. If he believed I was a worthy target then let him.

I heard him in the bedroom. He was creeping slowly. Too slowly.

My hand was ready with my gun.

Then I felt something sit on the bed, I fought myself not to react. I stirred only a little. My hand still clenched around my gun.

Something cold touched my face. Then it stopped. He stopped. Something had disturbed him. I had hoped he hadn't heard Jeffries or Barnett enter my flat. They wouldn't have closed the door; I had hoped they would close it over. But not shut it properly. I felt the weight shift from my bed, and I almost hissed.

He walked to the door. For once I was glad that my flat was in pitch darkness, as he wouldn't find Jeffries or Barnett.

He hadn't. He returned to my room. The something cold traced my face and then it traced down my chest.

He was preparing. Taking pleasure clearly.

That infuriated me. What a closet pervert!

Then it wasn't something cold. It was a gloved hand. He traced my face and then my chest. My hand tightened under the covers. He really was a pervert.

Then I felt something sharp hit my side. I gasped, swinging the gun out and firing in one motion. I felt something warm splatter me, and something warm trickled from my side. Then the pain hit, agonising pain. But I tried to ignore it, I was going to die if I concentrated on it.

"Bitch!" He growled and I saw something glint, before Barnett and Jeffries swung in, Jeffries launching himself at the suspect, handcuffing him.

Barnett ran straight to me, adding pressure to the wound, grabbing my dressing gown to let me keep my modesty.

It was over. He had been caught.

He had failed.

We had won.

Barnett was a godsend, having his hand on my side to keep pressure and with the other phoning 999. They arrived very quickly, along with my team, who helped Jeffries to take the murderer to the station.

Amy helped Barnett by relieving him, so that when the paramedics wheeled me out on a gurney, to take to hospital for immediate surgery. Barnett's face had gone a fire engine red. Clearly embarrassed.

The killer had only managed to puncture my stomach, and that was lucky really in the scheme of things. After a patch up under anaesthesia I would be fine. Just out of work for time while I rested and recuperated. Which the team was glad to do as well, they needed it.

The morning following my surgery, Barnett was sitting in my hospital room when I awoke.

"Barnett?" I asked.

"Your awake! That's good news." Barnett smiled, brandishing a small bunch of flowers. "I brought you flowers."

I thanked him. "You didn't have to."

"After last night, yes I think I did. You were so brave and amazing Mags." He blushed. "I'm sorry it caused you pain."

"Well, the ends justify the means as they say." I said, shifting a little. It was agonising. "Bill alright?"

"He's fine. Final touches on the case, closing it as you police folk say." He laughed.

I laughed and regretted it. Searing pain.

"Steady." Barnett said.

I looked at him. He genuinely seemed surprised and concerned that I was trying to sit up. I had a job to get to.

"Thank you, Barnett."

"I think we have gone past last names Mags, please call me Joe." Barnett-Joe said a small hint of a smile.

"I believe we have Joe." I smiled in response. "Why are you here Joe?"

"I quite enjoyed working with you and the police of course." Here Joe blushed. "I wanted you to know that I know my history of the Whitechapel area, so if you require assistance again, then please don't hesitate to contact me. Even it is a slight niggle of doubt."

"Thank you Joe, I shall bear that in mind when I am back on my feet." I smiled. "But here's hoping it will be a normal time in Whitechapel."

How wrong I would turn out to be.

Chapter 6

It was over two months later, I had been back on the force for restricted hours, having had Jeffries hovering like a hawk. Everyone had clapped the minute I had walked into the station. Painfully and slower than usual, but I still walked into the station.

"Ok, thank you, back to your duties." I waved and headed to my team's room. Here they clapped as I entered.

"Here comes the Abberline who caught the copycat Jack the Ripper." Jeffries joked. That had been the headline in the paper once it had been made clear who the copycat had been. His name had been given and his trial concluded in secrecy that he was guilty, being sentenced to life in jail.

"Oh Please, it wasn't just me though." I blushed a little. I wasn't used to this.

"No, but you're the first Abberline to do it." Said Max.

"Probably not the first Abberline to be stabbed on duty though." I joked.

The team laughed.

"Right," I breathed. "What's been going on while I have been bed bound." I sat down in an empty chair beside Bill's desk. I keep going back and forth between first and last names with Bill, on some hand he is the sergeant-Jeffries, but he is also the friend Bill. It gets confusing in my head, even mine as an Abberline.

"Not a lot Ma'am." Jack said quietly.

"Now, now Jack, I may have been stabbed but I am still Mags. Don't forget it."

"I won't Mags Ma'am, but it's been pretty quiet since we caught Dhipett." Dhipett being the name of the Jack the Ripper copycat.

"Well now Mags is back that's going to change." Max joked. No sooner had he said that, the phones rang.

Everyone groaned. I laughed. "Once more into the fray dear friends!" I called as I hefted myself to my feet and sluggishly headed to my office, where my sturdy chair awaited, amidst a mountain of paperwork.

Over a month passed.

We were nearing the Christmas period, with domestic violence being our only port of call. It was becoming mind-numbing. But I welcomed it after the hellish moments of hunting the Ripper copycat.

December seventh came around, and the team were celebrating Amy's twenty fifth. Although I never drank much, I came to acknowledge her as a well thought of member of the team and colleague. Every so often my side would make me hiss. Even though I was now fully healed. Physically anyway, mentally I still felt those cold touches of the knife and the rough hands, gloved, waking me in sweat -soaked sheets. I had been asked to speak to a therapist and I had, telling her that these nightmares would only ease with time. And they eventually did, until they were faint whispers in my dreams. His face mainly I saw disappear into shadows never to be seen again.

Amy, bless her was inebriated. Very much so hammered, it was a good thing today had been her day off and she wasn't due at the station until the following day as she had, like we all had some well-deserved time off. I envied her a little. Her youth. But then I remembered I had lived like her. At least I had tried to. It was hard with my family background; I was already the black sheep.

Jeffries-I had decided to refer him to in my head, name when I spoke to him, jolted me from my thoughts as he sat down.

"Well, back to it tomorrow." He said simply.

"Yes. How's Ann?" I asked.

"Good, a little relieved that everything has gone back to normal. Was always wondering if it had been me that would have been stabbed." He was still annoyed that our team hadn't been recognised as the ones that captured Ripper. In the eyes of the rest of the police, we were a rag tag bunch of failures, that would only change in time. Something we had plenty of.

That was until my phone rang.

"Abberline."

"Homicide."

"Ok, where?" I jotted down the name. Glanced at my watch. Half eleven pm. Well, looks like there is no rest for the wicked. I thought.

"Bill, homicide." I said, standing.

"What about the others?" He asked copying me.

"Get them sobered up. We're on duty as of now." I said, pulling on my coat before we jumped into a taxi to the scene of the crime.

The Highway, Whitechapel.

That was our destination. A tailor shop off the highway called Shadwell's. Apparently, we had been called because all within the shop had been murdered. Aside from one person.

Apparently, the person, Olivia Hatfield had been sent to go and get some late-night snacks for the rest of the workers. She had returned to the shop being locked and dark inside when they normally worked until the early hours of the morning. A shiver ran up my spine. It was happening again.

Why? Why now?

Hadn't we gone through enough?

Well, we got into the shop and the carnage that met us, was blood-soaked floors. Smashed in skulls and death. Mary was already on the scene, in overalls and gloves.

"Glad to see you Maggie." She said smiling at me.

"Glad to see you too Mary." I said, sighing, pulling on my own overalls and shoes, gloves and other forensic outfit pieces that was required. "Into the breach again?"

"I'm afraid so." She said with her own sad smile.

"What do we have?"

"Well the owner we have upstairs, his skull and throat cut. Luckily, he was a bachelor so no wife or children to count amongst the dead, only his workers. The youngest one'sdownstairs have all had their skulls caved in premortem and post-mortem, they had their throats cut."

"So, a little different to our mutilated victims, with the Ripper then."

"Very much so." Mary took us into one of the rooms. "Here we found a chisel." She said pointing out the object on the floor.

"Not the murder weapon though." I added.

"No, no blood or anything on it. Just laid beside the young man you see there."

"Do we know the names?"

"James Marxwell, Oliver Howards, Carwyn Adams." She pointed each dead individual in turn. "Guilty for nothing apart from being here and working here."

I looked at the young man in front of me, who still had so many years to live, to fall in love, marry and have children if that had been his choice. It created a lot of sadness. He instead was laying there dead, with no future.

"So how did this happen?" Jeffries asked.

"We are unsure. The young lady who also worked here, said that she had left the shop at ten thirty to run some errands and when she returned she thought they were playing a prank on her, until the officer that was on his rounds found her and entered the building. That's when he called it in." Mary continued. I took a good look at her. She had been aged by the Ripper copycat killings, so seeing this was bound to bring back some memories we all had forced out of our minds.

"Do we have another serial killer here?" I asked. Again, my gut was saying it was only beginning.

"Who knows, but I know one thing. This killer is like a ghost. There are no footprints. It was as if they came in, killed and vanished." Mary said doubt filling her voice.

We returned to the station after that, the rest of the team apart from Amy of course, was there, sobered and ready to hear what we had. I went straight for my office. I knew who we should contact straight away.

"Barnett." I knew he would answer.

"Detective Inspector Abberline." I smiled through the phone. Joseph Barnett, a historian on the Whitechapel and London area.

"Mags, what do I owe this pleasure to?" Barnett replied. I could tell he was smiling. I hadn't seen him since the morning after my surgery in the hospital.

"Murder of course." I chuckled slightly. "We have had a murder that has occurred in a tailor shop on the Highway."

"And your asking me for my help?" He asked.

"Of course, not making the same mistake as last time." I replied. That sobered me up. If we had, we probably would have caught the copycat much earlier and three of the women would be still alive.

"Of course, I will dig through my files and get back to you." Barnett replied.

"Thanks Joe."

We hung up and I went and joined my team at the whiteboards. They had been hard at work, usual for them.

Johnathon was busy phoning and Max was studying the whiteboards avidly.

Jack and Jeffries were missing. They must have been with the young lady who found the bodies, along with the police officer who had assisted her. Not needing me there, I walked over to the whiteboards, startling Max.

"Mags, Ma'am." He said.

"What do we have Max?" I asked, leaning on one of the tables.

"Well, the victims were in the middle of tailoring suits and outfits that several customers had brought in a week before, we have contacted them. We are also looking into whether the shop had any work completed on it, as the sergeant noticed new panels in the staircase, John is on that." Max paused. "Other than that, we don't have a lot to go on until the report comes in about the murder weapon."

"Good job." I smiled. "Know I can count on you all, sorry to have to sober you all up so quickly."

"No problems Mags, Ma'am." Max smiled. "We knew the job description when we joined the force."

I just smiled. I wish that I had when I had joined the force, at least then it would have prepared me for copycat murders that hadn't been seen since the 1800's. But now at least I wasn't a rookie in those matters anymore.

"Let's keep the momentum going. Find out what you can, tell Jeffries I am headed down to the morgue." I paused. "Unless you wish to join me Max?"

His face lit up like a fourth of July party. "Could I?"

I chuckled, "As long as you can keep your dinner and alcohol down, why not."

He jumped to it and we headed down, he was like an exuberant puppy.

We reached that dank and dark space, shivers going up my spine. It had been a regular occurrence when the Ripper copycat had been killing to visit this place. We were back there again. Very little to go on and multiple people dead.

"Hey Mary, any news?" Max asked. I had let him take a step forward. They all needed the experience if they wanted to get to becoming a Detective Inspector one day.

"Ah, Max, lovely to see you, you too Mags." Mary replied. "Yes, we were just about to phone up."

"So, what news do we have?" I asked, following on from Max's question.

"Well, it was a blunt instrument to the backs of the heads of all the victims causing depressed cranial fractures. So, something like a hammer or similar. We are still looking into the sizing, but I would imagine it would be either a blocking hammer or an electricians hammer."

"What's the difference?" I asked. I was not a handyman or woman for that matter, only resorting to doing my own DIY when the occasion called for it. I only owned the basic tool kit for those occasions.

"A blocking hammer is used by blacksmiths, known for their small frame and for detail. So that the blacksmiths can use on an anvil or a block, has a flat face and is known for finesse." Max said, glancing at me, "My brother works in a blacksmith as a volunteer." He continued. "An electrician's hammer is like a hammer that carpenters use, but has a claw, less pronounced, to grip onto fasteners. It is usually quite expensive as it has insulation built for shocks." He then glanced at me again. "My dad was an electrician, so when I wanted to know he told me."

"Well, at least one of us knows the difference." I laughed. I hadn't known a lot about Max. I had tried to.

"Yes, even I wouldn't know the difference." Mary laughed.

"So, we need to be on the lookout for one of those." I said. "Good job Mary, let us know if there is any difference once the sizing has come through." We waved as we left.

"Great work in their Max, since you know the differences, take either Jack or John with you to go on the hunt with the contractors hired for the upgrades." I said as we walked back into the team room.

Jeffries and Jack were back from talking to the young lady and the officer in question.

"Hi, what did find out?" I asked, noticing that Jeffries was writing on the whiteboard. Max went straight to John and set straight to work.

"The young lady was extremely entitled." Jack replied. "Reported that she always was bullied by the others and her boss. She had made harassment accusations to her boss, who she said always shrugged them off. She has shown regret about that all now, but still believed that it had nothing to do with her."

"Has she named anyone?" I asked.

"No, though we have looked into the boss's family. No siblings, no cousins. No-one there of interest." Jack said as Jeffries finished what he was writing.

"So, we got nothing." Jeffries said. "Nothing was taken from the shop's till, money that Shadwell had been storing in a safe had not been touched either."

"So, what's the motive?" I pondered. "Money clearly it isn't. Revenge? There's no evidence for revenge though."

"Could the motive be not being paid?" Jack questioned. "Are there any records of contractors not being paid?" He called over to Johnathon and Max.

"Nothing here. Contractors were all paid." Johnathon said. "But here's the thing, one of the contractors had some tools go missing, and apparently in the records that Shadwell kept, groceries were bought multiple times as if something was eating them before they could."

"Some sort of revenge for eating all the food. Seems like a pretty ridiculous reason for killing people." Jeffries scathingly said.

"Who knows. But John, Max, get out there and talk to the contactors, Jack give Amy a call and see how she is. We are going to need all hands-on deck as soon as possible." I ordered. All of them snapped to attention. Jeffries followed me into my office.

"Mags?" He asked sitting.

"I called Barnett, if he found anything similar in history, he was to let us know. It's like before Bill, my gut is saying this is familiar."

"I believe you Mags. After the copycat I trust you." Jeffries said.

<u>Chapter 7</u>

The next day, Barnett phoned.

"Detective Inspector Abberline."

"It's Joe. I found something." Barnett replied, I got my notepad ready to write down all his information.

"Go on Joe."

"It sounds as if you have another Ratcliffe Highway murder on your hands. Back in 1811, on the seventh of December, a maidservant was sent from Timothy Marr's draper shop to run some errands, while she was away the Marr family and their apprentice was murdered in the shop. When the maidservant couldn't gain access to the property, she called for a constable making his rounds, when he could rouse no-one from the property the neighbour awoke and offered his help, climbing over the fence he found the door unlocked at the back, he forced entry and found the four murdered. He let the constable in, and they discovered not only the husband and wife murdered but the seven-month-old child in its crib. All murdered, throats cut, and skulls smashed in."

I paused in my note taking. "Who did they find that could have done this? And what did they find as the weapon of murder?" I asked.

"A man by the name of John Williams, a sailor who was staying at the Pear Tree, he was found in his cell hanging. He was buried at the crossroads on the Highway. They found the murder weapon, a chisel and hammer."

"Similarities already, thanks Joe, let me know if you find anything else."

"I did, a similar case only twelve days later. Another family was found dead, so expect that. It was at a tavern in on New Gravel's Lane. This was a short distance from the first murder. People gathered because a man climbed near naked from a second window on bedding, crying they are being murdered. The man was a lodger, and the crowd forced open the tavern's doors, the owner, his wife and a maid were found murdered the same way. Throats cut and their skulls smashed in. The wife's throat had been cut down to the neck bone. John Williams was also found guilty of these murders." Barnett continued.

"So we expect another family to be murdered, unless we find our killer- who unlike John Williams actually has committed this crime."

"Yes,"

"Is that all Joe?"

"Yes if I find anymore I will call."

"Thanks Joe." We hung up and I took those notes to the others.

"We should be on the lookout for another murder in eleven days. Barnett called. Similarities between our case and the Ratcliffe Highway murders of 1811. Two survivors each time." I looked up from my notes. Max and Jack had their mouths open. "Another copycat, yes. Anyway, keep an eye out for what the tavern called the King's Arms on New Gravels Lane is now, as that was where the second bunch of murders occurred."

"I know where that is!" Max said. "It's a student house now." He double checked his notes, "It's also one of the buildings the contactors worked on that worked on Shadwell's."

"Get over there, look for anywhere that could be a hiding place."

Max went straight out.

"Jeffries?"

"Yes Mags Ma'am?"

"I want you with me. We need to talk to that girl again."

We called the young woman into an interrogation room.

"You've already spoken to me." She said arrogantly. "I told you everything."

"New evidence has come to light." I said simply. "Did any food go missing?"

"Food? Yes, a bunch of stuff, Shadwell thought someone was eating it all and got quite angry at us workers, thinking we were stealing it." The girl said.

I glanced at Jeffries. "So, is that why you were sent out that night?" I asked her.

"Yes, Shadwell wanted me to grab some bread and some cheese to take over from the stuff that had been eaten." The girl's face fell. "I have to thank him though, he saved me from being killed by doing that." She paused on the verge of tears. "And all I did was belittle him for not helping with being bullied." Regret.

"Do you know the names of all the contractors that came to work at Shadwell's?" I asked.

"Yes, one of them was really creepy. Caught him staring at us all when he should have been working." The girls face screwed up in disgust. "His name was Ellis, Ellis Shields."

I saw Jeffries write his name down.

"Were there any others?" I prodded.

She thought. "David Howe, Jace Theobald." They were the main ones, but I just remember Ellis more, he was creepy and seemed to pop out when we least expected him. Like he was a ghost."

"Thank you, we will be in touch." I said.

"Thanks, could I ask one thing?" The girl said.

"Of course."

"When you catch the person who did this ask them why? Why that shop? We have done nothing to anyone." She started to cry. "All I want is for someone to tell me that."

She left. Once she had left Jeffries and I looked at one another.

"Ellis Shields." Jeffries muttered. "I know that name from somewhere."

"Hmm." I simply said.

"What you are thinking?" Jeffries asked.

"If Ellis Shields also worked on the student house. Also, how he seemed to pop out of nowhere." I tapped my chin.

"Mags Ma'am!" Jack burst into the room. "You need to see this!"

We glanced at one another and ran after him.

A newspaper sat on the team's desk. The headline was: **Ghost murders tailor!**

Again, the team and I glanced at each other. I read the paper. It linked that something supernatural had killed the people at Shadwell's. And not a person in living flesh. I glanced at Jeffries.

"Find the author of this and find his source." I said, I was angry. This would stir the public into a frenzy and if we weren't careful there would vigilantes on the hunt for this supernatural being, causing more fatalities than we were working towards preventing. I tried not to show my anger in my voice, but I knew that Jeffries was also angry.

"Right away Ma'am." Max said. He knew from my tone how serious this was. And he got straight to it, phoning the paper straight away.

Jeffries and I looked at one another. We had to find this killer and find them we would. We knew that this was no spook, this was a flesh and blooded person.

Later that night, I had broken my no smoking rule. I had taken a cigarette and went outside into the air. I needed to think. I needed to think without distractions. The team was running around following up leads and I needed to think clearly, where a shut door would not help. Why was this happening again? Why was this a test of my ability to solve murders? Why couldn't I have one normal murder?

If any murder was normal...

I took a deep drag on the cigarette and thought. Someone who was able to pop out of nowhere did sound supernatural, but there must be a logical explanation. There was one but it just wasn't clear. Well at that moment anyway.

There had to be!

Luckily my team had found the author of the article in the paper, had found the source and it turned out that someone had overheard what the girl had said on the scene and had spun it into a crazy supernatural story.

That didn't stop us from asking them to retract the story from the paper and asking them to hold off for calling to arms vigilantes, who we found that were beginning to appear in the streets, to find this supernatural being. Max and Jack had run into a few after heading to some contractors to find Ellis Shields. They came out unscathed, but it could have been much, much worse.

The vigilantes were vicious and ruthless. They were stopping people they considered a supernatural in the street and beating them up. Many officers were being called out to deal with it. It was utter madness.

This continued for some time until the government put out a statement telling everyone that vigilantes were not needed as the police force were close to capturing the flesh and blood villain.

It died down but didn't completely vanish overnight. Vigilantes still combed the streets but in lesser numbers.

Until the night of the nineteenth of December, that was. We were at the local food truck, all of us including Amy who had been clued into the situation. We were near where the student accommodation was, still no closer to catching the suspect, who we believed was Ellis Shields. It was finding him that was the tricky part, he had gone AWOL from work and home. No-one had seen him, a few of us were going to walk around the student accommodation once eating and see if we could spot him from outside.

A girl passed us mumbling about everyone eating her things and that she was sick of it, and Jeffries and I believed that she had come from the accommodation. I asked Amy and Johnathon to tail her. It was likely that she was going to be the only survivor. Jeffries, Max and Jack and I were off to the accommodation. Outside it was quiet, Max and Jack went around the back and Jeffries and I hung around the front.

That was when we heard him.

"They're being murdered!" We glanced up and without a moment of pausing we broke the door down.

Inside was Ellis Shields, he saw us in mid stroke of killing and ran. Dropping the murder weapon but we followed him, he had ducked out the back, and we heard a scuffle. I knew that Max and Jack had him. I called in the murder. Luckily, he had only managed to kill one of the students, the others cowered.

When the girl came back, she was shocked, dropping the milk that she had clearly gone out to buy.

The milk sloshed over her shoes, but she didn't care. She saw her friend lying on the rug in front of the broken-down door. And that was when she screamed. A high piercing scream that went right through me and I knew that my ancestor probably heard it and rolled in his grave. I fought the urge to put my hands over my head and block the noise. But in the end Jeffries escorted her out so I could finish calling it in. The other students came out hiding and went and joined their friend outside while we waited, the tears flowing well from their eyes. How close they had come to being murdered in cold blood.

We arranged for alternative accommodation for them for tonight, so we could get the forensics report from the house, find Shield's hiding spot and border it up. When we did, we were shocked. It was like a priest hole used to hide people who were of Protestant faith back in the fifteenth century. It also explained why food had been going missing. He had been staying in the houses he had helped renovate. Eating the food in fridges and cupboards.

Max and Jack had taken Shield's to be locked away in a cell. Filing the reports while they waited for us back at the station.

The knife and the hammer we put in the evidence locker at the station, congratulating Max and Jack for their efforts in catching Shield's outside.

We were in the team room when almighty cry came from the cell blocks.

I rushed straight down there, afraid on what I would find.

My worst nightmare.

Shield's had hung himself, using the shirt off his back, clearly copying John William's supposed suicide.

I crumpled to the floor. Not caring who saw. Our only suspect and our only killer gone.

We would be a laughingstock after this, more than what we already were.

Chapter 8

There were no other words for it. Shell shock. That's what the team was feeling. After our success, well nothing seemed to be going right.

First our amazing capture of the killer, his then suicide and now we were being mocked. All the station, but we blanked them, at least I did. The youngsters took it a little to heart. People in the street also mocked our actions.

I smoked more and more each day. I always wondered why. Why. Why, why did he kill himself?

Did he realise there was no way out? He had been caught red handed after all. Was death the better option?

I didn't have an awful amount of heart left. Each day passed with more long hours that led to questions from our Chief of Police. Questions I couldn't always answer. And when I did, he got angry. I was truthful, that was the sad part.

Jack and Max, it hit harder. They had caught him; they had searched him. But clearly, they didn't factor that he would use his own clothes to kill himself, no-one sane could. They followed protocol exactly. But to the rest of the world, they hadn't done enough. So, they were currently on compassionate leave, though we knew it was a suspension. Amy had been moved to desk duty as had Johnathon, Jeffries and I, well we had been given a limited suspension. We still had to do our jobs. That was the hard part. Doing this as just the two of us. It made our jobs harder, just like it had been intended.

We had been that way, kept our heads lowered, kept to the work we were handed, when the arrival of a new case had been brought to us. No other department could handle it, it would seem.

A foot had been found, carried by a fox. In Whitechapel the odds of a fox finding a foot that had been decomposing for some time, is not common, so we were called in. All of us.

A small reunion and then we were straight back onto it.

I went down to the morgue by myself. Mary smiled at me sadly, she was aware of what had been going on.

"What happened do we think Mary?" I droned.

"Well, it has decomposed well. Still unsure, it could be hours old it could be months." Mary sighed. "We have nothing. Apart from the fact it has spent some time in the earth and in the water."

"Thanks anyway Mary."

"If you find her head, then we can go from there."

"Her head?" I asked, shock appearing in my voice. "What makes you think it's a her?"

Mary pointed to the ankle. There on the ankle was a faded tattoo, and then I looked again at the foot. Daintier than a mans and thinner. Another woman murder. I sighed. I really hated this job sometimes.

On the return to the team, I had to pause. I needed a cigarette. Instead, I went inside and told them the little information we had.

The only option was to find where the fox had found it, and to search the river.

Dejected that was the only word for it.

As I smoked a cigarette, the team deciding to scope the areas with lots of earth, where foxes could live and the other half looking on the river with another police team. I had a thought. Why? What was it about this year that was causing all these murders? And not just normal, if there was anything as a normal murder.

It was tough.

There could have been anything in the river, we just didn't know what to look for, and it wasn't just our team, it was the other team as well. We had nothing yet again.

I decided to walk along the river, alone this time. Then I saw a black plastic bag. The sounds of water hitting against something hard, something that I was a little hoping for. On using gloves to open it, I called for my team. "Got something!" And then I recoiled.

A leg. I had found a leg.

I had been moved away from the area, while forensics were called to take it back to the morgue. I stood out of the way, beside our unmarked police car. I was smoking, I had just had a huge shock, not expecting to find something that huge.

While I stood there, I contemplated whether I should call Barnett.

"Call." Came Jeffries voice from seemingly nowhere, until I looked to my left.

"Hmm?"

"Call Barnett, he would know of many cases, at least we would have a starting point." He continued. "Which is better than nothing in this case."

"True." Sighing I stumped out my cigarette, pulled out my mobile and dialled his number.

"Joseph Barnett."

"Joe its D.I Abberline."

"Hi Mags, what can I do for you?"

"We've found a foot and a leg, has there been any murders involving dismemberment?"

"I'll go through my files as soon as possible; I am just having a quick cuppa and will be right onto it." Barnett replied.

"Thanks Joe, good luck searching, let us know what you find."

"As always Mags, as always." We hung up.

"He's going to have a look through his files."

"Good, a start, we need to find out if there was anything else to do with that leg and foot. Whether they are from the same person or heaven forbid multiple people."

I knew Jeffries was right somehow. We had another copycat, but the question was, who and why?

We found out not that long after we returned to the station. The forensics had scanned the body parts and had come up with an answer.

"If you found a torso, it could help us determine how these souls died." Plural. So, we have a multiple number of bodies. I thought as Mary continued.

"Bodies yes, women yes." Mary paused. "Not just women though, women of a certain age, which is hard considering the condition the body parts are in."

"So, we are looking at someone who kills women, dismembers them." I said. Jeffries scoffed. "So, another copycat do we think?"

"Most likely what with everything that has been going on." Mary sighed. "What is going on with the world?"

"If I had any idea Mary, I would tell you." I said, patting her shoulder and leaving.

It seemed that another murderer was out in Whitechapel.

This one had clearly been killing for some time, we just had not been aware of the bodies. So, the team and I were looking into missing person cases, from anywhere to months ago. Another starts due to no leads.

We were pursuing those with the help of the missing persons teams, considering they had, had no luck finding them until this case surfaced. They had hoped working with the apparently pitiful, failure and pathetic homicide team would see that they could find these missing people. They saw in full effect how much we weren't failures. Just how little of the case we had at the start, to where we had. Max was quite chatty considering that these same people had been mocking us. He was chatting to a young lady by the name of Emily, one of the missing people's team. She had asked about the Ripper case, the Hider (the Shield's case) and now this one. She seemed genuinely shocked when Max had told her what little on each of the cases we had, and how eventually we had managed to solve them. I had my back to them by using the information given to put on a separate whiteboard, but I clearly saw out of the corner of my eye some stares, not the normal glares but stares of admiration. It made me smile inwardly, finally we were being seen as anything but disgraces to the police force, it showed them all what little we had to work with and how we managed. Hopefully the message would pass on to other departments and there would be unity within the police station.

After some time, it seemed longer than what it was, we managed to grab a few missing women that had not been seen. We contacted the parents and asked whether they had been seen near the river area. Four had been another had finally contacted her mother, saying she had run off with a friend to live in Brighton. So that one we could cross off our list.

"We have a potential four people." I concluded. The large team in front of me were taking notes. "Hetty, Henrietta Gravels, Grace Hewes, Lucy Theano and Jane Fright." I pointed to each of them in turn. "These four were last seen a few months ago. And by the state of the decomposition we have of the body parts mingled with time in the water, this is likely the people we have to find." Shocked faces. "So, we need to tail their last movements, find who they were with and where they were. If we do that then we have a chance to find out who their killer is." I paused, mentally tallying who we had minus the missing people, who would be doing house runs. "Split in two and take two each. The report back here." Quick glance at a watch. "Four pm. Make sure you take ten-minute breaks." I pointedly made the point of making sure that they ate. "Off we go team!"

My team cheered and raced off to do just that. That was when I noticed the head of the missing person's department. "George, what are you doing here?" I asked.

"Came to see the failings in action." He sneered. Then the sneer dropped. "And what I saw isn't a failing, it's making sure you follow what you have, making sure that your team is looked after as well." He shifted. "I apologise for the actions of me and my team. Any help we will be glad to help."

"Thanks George, I will be sure to do just that." I smiled slightly. "Now, I am sorry, but we have lots to do."

"No problem." He left.

Things had started to look up. We just needed to find this killer, and those women's bodies. That couldn't be that hard could it?

But it turned out to be just that.

With a search party down by the docks and in the forests, we managed to bring more body parts, more body parts that could potentially be four women. Four women that we could give back to their families, so they could grieve. That was the focus, to get them back to their parents.

And we had managed to find two out four torsos. One had a tattoo on the shoulder, which we linked to the foot. We also managed to figure out who's body that was as well. It was Lucy Theano.

But we had found no heads. That was the problem. No heads meant that there was no real way of identifying the bodies. We had to find them. On the positive note Mary had something.

"They were poisoned."

"How can you be sure?"

"We ran the tests for the usual poisons and then this came up." She showed us a substance that had been revealed from finding Lucy Theano's torso.

"Tetrodotoxin?" Jeffries asked.

"Mainly found in puffer fish, poisonous dart frogs and the blue ringed octopus." Mary said triumphantly.

"So, he used this poison on the girls. But how would you get this poison in the UK?" I asked.

"Unless someone is keeping a puffer fish, dart frog or a blue ringed octopus as a pet and extracting the toxin, I would have no idea, they are not native to the UK." Mary said.

I glanced at Jeffries, we seemed to have the same thought.

"So, we look into what these things eat and whether anyone has bought a specific tank for those creatures."

"Afraid so." Mary said. "It's not much I know, but I am trying."

"We know Mary, we know." I smiled.

We headed back up and I took Jeffries to the side before we went into where the team were busy hard at work.

"Mags?"

"I'm concerned."

"About the poison?"

"No about our team."

He looked at me and I could see the concern reflected in his eyes.

"Me too Mags, me too."

We headed in. The team looked up, the question in their eyes, had we found anything new?

"Right, they were poisoned." I said.

"Tetrodotoxin. Look for places that sell tanks for exotic animals, specifically for a fish, frog or an octopus." I simply said. "Someone is clearly harvesting the toxin to use on these women, for whatever reason. We find them, the sooner this ends."

The team went straight on that. I took a good look at them all. The bags under tired eyes, the drawn and pinched faces. The worry, the shakes, the sipping coffee in between researching. We needed this to end and soon. I probably looked no different.

Chapter 9

The search parties had found three more torsos. More limbs but still no heads. All in the same states of decomposition. If any body parts were missing it was because they had been either eaten or been pulled out to sea, where we could not get them, at least that's what the coastguard had told us. For some of those families, that would be all they would receive. A torso and a few limbs in order to grieve their children. The women were all young, in their early twenties. That we had discovered as much. All the women had been missing, and the parents were still unsure of whether they were their child, until we found the heads. No heads were found, perhaps the killer was using them as a kind of trophy, but no sane person would have a head in their living room; whoever we were dealing with, had to be keeping them somewhere. Just not in plain sight.

"D.I Abberline."

"Mags, it's Joe."

"Joe?"

"Sorry it has taken so long. But I have found a couple of files. The Marquis de Sade and-"

"Joe, is any of the files mention poisoning?"

He was quiet for some time and I heard papers rustling.

"Poisoning? That's new. Well not too new but still."

"Sorry with everything going on I haven't had time to update you."

"That's understandable Mags." He rustled some more. "How were the bodies discovered." He finally asked.

"Dismembered and thrown in the sea or river we feel." Another pause. More rustling.

"Have their heads been found?" He asked again. Clearly, he was looking through the files he had collected, using the information he had been given.

"How did you know?" I asked. "No, they haven't yet."

"So, a trophy or something else." He muttered talking to himself. More rustling, and urgent sounds. "Ok so, The Marquis De Sade, he did poison, but dismemberment was not his forte. It sounds like the Thames Torso Killer, but also it could be…" He trailed off, still trying to find the information. "Keats! That's it!" He exclaimed.

"Keats? The poet?" I asked.

"Yes, he wrote a poem about Isabella and the Basil pot." Barnet explained. "She killed her lover and placed his head inside a pot on a shrine, where she would drape her hair over the pot so it looked like basil."

"So, the killer is keeping them as a trophy but in a pot! But that doesn't explain the bodies being dismembered and poisoned." I added.

"And that would be why you haven't found the heads!" Barnett sounded excited in a weird way.

"Hmm…" I thought. "Our killer, could they be acting some kind of revenge?"

Barnett rustled papers. "That is not uncommon. What was the poison?" He asked.

"Tetrodotoxin."

A rustle. "There is nothing about using that in a revenge crime. Perhaps...no that's ludicrous."

"What Joe?" Sitting up, I had realised that maybe Barnett was onto something.

"It's ludicrous Mags."

"Tell me anyway. It could be something to look into."

"Well, say that it was revenge, perhaps it is because they don't understand the poison they are using. Maybe they wanted to do something else. Maybe they wanted the victims to be in love with them, instead of the aphrodisiac they were looking for they grabbed the wrong type of animal to use."

I pondered for a moment. He had a point.

Barnett continued. "So, they clearly wanted these women to be in love with them, thus keeping the heads, an act of bizarre love, but when the poison killed them instead of being the aphrodisiac they wanted, they had to hide the bodies. So, dismembering them, and tossing them as pieces has hid the killing. And because they don't understand the poison, it kept happening."

"That would explain the lull now. Perhaps the killer is researching now?"

"Yes, it would. So, really you need to look for someone who has had multiple people in their vicinity and last saw our victims."

"Thanks Joe, that's what we will do. Thanks again you have been a huge help." We hung up, finally somewhere else to go with.

Potentially someone who has been seen with all four women, or last seen them. That may be a potential killer. So, we would have to have that list of people who have last seen the people, they may then appear on the list for buying a tank for a fish, frog or octopus. That would be our killer.

So, together, we collated the people from both lists, listed the names that appeared on both on the whiteboard. Those were the people we were going to contact and visit. If one of them had even one of the suspected items, either a tank with an unusual fish, frog or had multiple pots that looked as though they were newly bought then they were to be brought in and questioned. Then we would find our killer.

Jeffries and I decided that we were going to go and question Jack Giles, a young man who worked and owned a sweet shop in the lower end of Whitechapel. It was a quiet and pleasant area. "Not too far from the river." I mused to Jeffries.

"Hmm." Jeffries said. "Nice little place too."

It was a small sweet shop. Located well and on the corner of the street. It was an emerald green with white lettering saying Ye Olde Sweet Shoppe. And the odd thing about it was that it was closed, despite opening times being on the door. That was suspicious. We hammered on the door, a young lady came from the downstairs area that looked like a basement from where we were. We asked her to open the door, so she did.

"Can I help you?" She asked.

"Jack Giles, we are looking for him." We flashed her our badges.

"He's upstairs, tending to his plants." She responded and looked fearful when we asked.

"Were you with him?"

"No, I was downstairs taking inventory." She replied, looking from me to Jeffries.

"Wait outside." We said in unison. She did as she was asked. I motioned to her to close the door behind her. Then Jeffries called

"Jack Giles, it's the police we have come to ask you some questions." Nothing came from above. Grabbing my gun, I started to walk up the stairs with Jeffries in front, doing the same. When we reached the top of the stairs, muffled movements came from the kitchen area, Jeffries motioned I go into the living room and scope that out while he went into the kitchen, he had agreed, me being stabbed once was enough.

I nodded, motioning to my ears should he need me. What awaited me in the living room, shocked me, but not so much when I heard Jeffries yell.

"No!" And I rushed in. Giles had cut his own throat. "Call it in." I said hoarsely and went back to the living room.

The table was laid out like a dinner date, chocolates in the centre. I sniffed but could detect no unfamiliar smells. That must be how he poisoned them. Then another look I discerned a tank, that held a poisonous puffer fish. The poison we needed. Then I saw the flowers. Pictures taken of flowers in a graveyard on a grave. I knew where the women's heads were. Snatching the picture, I ran down the stairs, calling to Jeffries. He would wait until the ambulance arrived, with forensics, we had found our man. And it seemed as though we were just in time, before he had yet another victim. The poor girl was going to be his latest victim. I raced to the graveyard calling Mary as I went. Told her I had found the victims heads. I found the graveyard St Patrick's Cemetery, not more than two or three roads from the sweet shop and searched for the grave. When I found it, I blanched, laying in front on me was Marie Jeanette Kelly's grave. Right beside it was a small bunch of flowers that had been planted next to it. Grave number sixty-six, row sixty- six, plot number ten. The flowers were red Poppies and yellow Hyacinths.

I called Barnett from there. "Joe?"

"Mags, what's going on?"

"I found the women's heads, but you will never guess where they are. Do you know what red poppies and yellow hyacinths mean?"

"You mean in the language of Victorian flowers?" He asked, he sounded perplexed. "Why where are you?"

"St Patrick's Cemetery. Row sixty-six, grave number sixty-six plot number ten." I said breathlessly.

"St Patrick's?" A gasp. "Mary Jane Kelly?"

"You know your history well." I said, my voice croaking. "What do those flowers mean?"

"Two minutes, I shall look it up on the web." Clicks and clacks were heard. I just stared. I had come full circle. Why? Why here? "Mags? The Red Poppies stand for Pleasure and the yellow Hyacinths, they stand for jealousy." My breath caught. "Mags? Are you alright?"

"Fine," I breathed. "So, this suspect was he jealous of the pleasure that Mary Jane Kelly received or was he jealous of the pleasure the Ripper gained from killing her?"

"It could be either Mags. But why don't you ask- "

"He's dead. He killed himself, slit his own throat." I was hyperventilating, I could hear it. My words came fast and breathless.

Silence met my words.

"Mags, this is all too much to be coincidence." Barnett said quietly. "This all too strange."

"I agree Joe." I could hear the panic in my voice.

"Are you alone?" Barnett asked, somewhat fearful.

"Yes, at the moment." I gasped. "Why?"

"Someone could be watching." I felt the hairs on my arms raise at his words, Goosebumps and shivers wracked my body.I refused to glance around me.

"What makes you say that?" I said quieter, so only Barnett would hear.

"Well, I don't know. The fact that you have come there, you were stabbed, you were chosen to be Mary Jane Kelly by the Ripper copycat and now you're at her grave? Your being watched, someone who has known you." Barnett whispered. "But only those on the team and myself know the true ins and outs of the case, and even I only know what you have told me." I had to agree. "Be careful Mags." He whispered again before we said goodbye.

I called Mary, asking her where she was. "I am at the crime scene. Just finishing loading up the body. I won't be long."

"Can you ask Jeffries to come to St Patricks Cemetery as soon as he can please. Plot number ten, row sixty-six, grave sixty-six. Please. Hurry." I breathed. She reassured me that they would be there as soon as possible.

In ten minutes, Jeffries came bounding around the corner, gun ready to fire until he saw me. The expression on my face must have alerted him to what had sort of gone on. "Mags?" He questioned. I merely pointed to the grave in front of me.

Waited as his eyes read the name on the grave.

His look of terror mirrored mine.

"Mags, are you?" He didn't finish his sentence. I felt the blood had drained from my face.

"No. No I am not." I finished. As Barnett had said, this was not a coincidence. Something was going on.

Chapter 10

I didn't remember Mary arriving at the Cemetery.

I didn't remember the unearthing of the young women's heads.

I don't remember saying anything.

I don't remember getting back to the station.

I do remember, being sat in my office, with a cup of tea and Jeffries sitting opposite me, his mouth moving but I couldn't hear the words. Never in my whole career had I ever been shaken up so much. There had been cases before that had thrown me but none like this. My hands shook around the cooling mug of tea. Tentatively I took a sip.

That's when my hearing came back. "Mags?"

"Sorry Bill." I said hoarsely. I hadn't spoken since the cemetery.

"No need to apologise Mags." He sipped his coffee. "It clearly has shaken you. Perhaps you should go home?"

I shook my head fiercely. And gulped my tea down. Going home would not help, not where I could dwell on my thoughts and come up with theories and scare myself into oblivion. Plus, if what Joe said was true, someone or something was watching me. It knew my movements, whatever that was.

"Ma'am?" Jack peered his head into the office. "Some of us are headed out, the files are all logged, all the information is on the system now. Would you like to join us?"

Jeffries nodded at me at the corner of my eye.

"Of course, Jack, just give me a few minutes to get sorted and I shall meet you out front." I smiled.

I was glad I joined them, they looked as though they needed a pick me up, and the fact that their superior joined them said a lot about them and us as a team. They were worried about me, that much was clear. Clearly, when I had returned in my state it had thrown them all. I was usually the steadfast one, the one who was logical, scientific. But seeing where we had ended up today, well that was a shock to the system, I attuned it to being because of the trauma of being stabbed by the Ripper copycat. Although they had a drink I sat there with my Pepsi, watching the bubbles as I listened to their conversations, answering when they directed those conversations at me. Though my mind was still back at that grave. Why her of all people? Why me of all people?

And why did it feel like the Gates of Hell had been opened? What was the accomplishment of opening them now?

As I returned to my home, walked back by Jack and Max, I realised I had never paid too much attention to my home since the Ripper copycat. It seemed like a stranger's home. The pictures on the walls, the wallpaper, the furniture, it all seemed that I was in a stranger's home. I took my coat off, hanging it by the door, which I promptly locked, and chain bolted. I was still full of tremors over that incident. I just didn't want to admit it aloud.

As I opened my pack of cigarettes shakily, lighting on the balcony and inhaling the smoke, I closed my eyes. Listening to the night's song. People shouting and singing in the pub down the road, couples chatting happily on the street below, hearing the chirp of a nocturnal animal, somewhere down below me. The scents of woodsmoke, someone was burning firewood, the smells of the trees around me, shedding their final blossoms, even at this time of year. The smell of bleach, of disinfectant, from a home above me who was being thoroughly cleaned. All soothed my soul. These were familiar. Familiarity was reliable. Familiarity was home. Familiarity was safety. I exhaled, not realising I had held the cigarette smoke for so long, I watched the colourless smoke lazily waft in circles around me. And then I finished the cigarette.

There, much calmer. I hadn't realised how much I just needed a reminder of what was safe, secure and above all nontoxic, ironic despite the toxins I had just inhaled.

That was when I realised more than anything, I needed sleep. So, I did, not bothering to change, I fell on top of my bedclothes and instantly as soon as my head hit the pillow, slept in what felt like the first time in months. It was a dreamless sleep, that I felt too soon that I had woken up from.

I showered, again what felt like the first time in months, letting the warm spray hit my face. It was refreshing. Soothing. Like the winter's rain that fell like tears from the sky. I closed my eyes and just enjoyed the feeling.

When I had finished, drying myself and pulling on a fresh change of clothes I realised, that I hadn't felt like this since the Ripper copycat. I felt more like myself. The logical, scientific, rational me, that didn't believe in the supernatural or Hell. The me who believed that all things could be figured out, just needed time to do it. With renewed vigour I opened my door, grabbing my coat, keys, and the emergency packet of cigarettes just in case, almost jumped down the stairs two at a time, surprisingly not breaking a bone. And was on my way to work, grabbing some food for myself and for the rest of the team on my way.

Reaching the station, I hadn't even realised that I had reached it, I was walking on air. Refreshed and full of life. I am sure that my team would also notice the difference.

That was until I walked into the room and noticed the state it was in.

I froze in my tracks.

It had been trashed, that was the only way to describe it. How had it gotten that way?

Jeffries looked dumbfounded. I was sure he had said he would lock up last night, otherwise I wouldn't have left with the team. And he was a man of his word.

"Bill?" I said tentatively, "What's gone on?"

"I don't know! It wasn't like this when I locked up last night." I believed him.

"Then how?" I spotted our whiteboards, smeared with a handprint. Or what seemed to be a handprint. All over our hard work, luckily that had been written in a report and filed on the system before we left. "Who could have done this?" I asked.

"Whoever it was, was able to go through a locked door." Max said. "You and Sarg. Mags, Ma'am are the only ones with keys."

"I went home last night." I said. Max and Jack nodded

"We walked Mags, Ma'am back to her place."

"I went home, Ann was there."

"So, who could it have been?" We said in unison.

"Have you lost the keys at any point?" Amy said methodically.

"No." I said, and Jeffries just shook his head. "We would never be so careless."

"Sorry Ma'am, finding a rational explanation." Amy held up her hands. I wasn't accusing her. She knew that just using the brain she had been blessed with.

"No worries Amy." We all looked at one another. Just when we had seemingly gotten back to normal, there was the extra-ordinary waiting for us.

I did not like it one bit.

Soon, the tidying taking most of the morning, I managed to fall into my sturdy office chair, that is when I noticed them.

The flowers.

Sitting wrapped in a bouquet, fancy and pretty with a little note on it. I eyed the note as if it was about to come alive and bite me like a serpent. But when it did neither, I took it gingerly and opened it.

Ma'am,

The world to an end shall come, in eighteen hundred and eighty-one.

When HEMPE is soon, England's done,

Thy know me, thy see me but thy doesn't recognise me.

Will't I roam amongst fair Londinium for thou't fear me.

And it was unsigned.

I threw it onto my desk. Instead I pulled up the browser on my computer.

I typed in the first line, up came information on a woman named Mother Shipton, I recognised that name, I had completed a piece of history coursework based around the prophecies of Ursula Shipton, a supposed witch, back in my long-forgotten youth. The second line also came up in that search as well. So, the first two lines were prophecies from Mother Shipton, but the last two lines came up with nothing clear. They linked to Shakespeare, but nothing that was recognisable. I would have to try and work that out for myself.

"Thy know me, thy see me but thy doesn't recognise me. What could that even mean?" I pondered. "Will't I roam amongst fair Londinium for thou't fear me? Will't could be if in Shakespearean, so if I walked amongst Londinium? What is Londinium?" I typed in Londinium into the search engine, and it was the old name for London back in AD 43 when the Romans settled in Great Britain. "If I walked in London, for you? Would fear me?" I mused. "Does that mean if I walked in London, you would fear me?" I mused talking to myself aloud. That made no sense. No rational sense anyway.

I sat back heavily in my chair; I was getting exasperated at these riddles. Especially, riddles that made little to no sense.

"Mags, everything ok?" Jeffries said from my doorway. He noticed the flowers. "Who they from?" He asked.

"I don't know but whoever left them, must have trashed the room, and they left a message that is shrouded in nonsense." I said, rubbing my face with my hands.

"Can I see?" He asked. I handed him the note. I watched his mouth move with the words. His face furrowed as he thought. "What the hell does that mean?" He said.

"The first two lines are prophecies from a woman who was treated as a witch, the last two lines make no sense." I said. "I thought they meant if I walked in London, then you would fear me. But still, who would I fear that much if they walked the London streets?"

He looked at me, he could see no fear, only irritation. That was all I was projecting. Fear?! It was laughable. I feared no one. Well, no one at that point in time. I did feel fear, but never let it rule me, at least I tried not to let it.

"You should just bin it, Mags, seems like a waste of time if you ask me." Jeffries concluded. I agreed with him and threw it into my bin, forgetting about it.

And forget about it I did...until our next case came almost pelting through the door.

Chapter 11

The call came in late that night. I was in the office, reading some case files.

"D.I Abberline."

"There's been a murder."

"Ok, where?" I noted down the address, thanked the person on the other side, hung up and grabbed my coat, calling Jeffries and the others as I went.

"We got one."

Jeffries and I went straight to the car, this time I drove. I liked driving, allowed for concentration on the road only and not on other things. Allowed the mind to clear.

An abandoned warehouse. That was our destination.

"Why are we here?" Jeffries yawned.

"Apparently a homeless person was murdered on the top floor." I said, parking the car and climbing out, Jeffries following suit. Forensics were already here, photographing and making notes of how the body was found. We put on the full-length attire, shoes and climbed our way to the top floor. It was an old building, most places had caved in, it was eerie, dusty and I swore there were rats. We made sure to watch our steps on the rickety stairs that looked as though they were going to cave at any moment and regained our breath at the top. Once there the murder was obvious.

A noose had been hung from a rafter; the night sky clear in the gap that the roof showed. And on the other end of that noose hung our victim. Hands were tied behind their back, a cloth bag over their head. They were swinging, it looked as though they had been placed on a block of stones and then the stones had been removed from underneath them. A way to kill that broke the neck and caused strangulation. Mary was there, directing her team. Numbers littered the floor where they had found items, photographs were being taken, the flashes cutting through the gloom like lightning.

"Ok Mary, what do we have?" I asked. Knowing Jeffries was still recovering from the climb.

"Strangulation. But not self-inflicted." Mary said. It wasn't as gruesome as some of other cases and it was a slight relief. I had, had enough of those for a lifetime.

"So, a second person was involved. They must have strung him up and then pushed the rocks to kill them." Jeffries panted.

"Yes, it seems that way. We found the positioning of the stones to make it look like gallows, we also found the victims ID sitting over in the corner as if the suspect threw it away. A wallet is there as well, nothing inside apart from a picture." Mary said morosely.

"Do we know if the victim was brought here or came here willingly?" I asked.

"Willingly to a point. On the stairs there are two sets of footprints. One up and down, one just up. The first must have been the suspect, the second our victim here." Mary pointed.

"Has the bag been removed at all?" Jeffries asked, "So we can see the poor bugger to match to the ID?"

"No, we were waiting for you." Mary replied. "The cloth bag must have been added before the strangulation, but how the suspect managed to get it over the victim and tie them in the noose we are unclear. There is some blood over by the stones, so they must have been set up before our victim arrived."

"So, our killer either knew our victim or knew he or she was coming here." I pondered.

"Alright." Said a male on Mary's team, Jared I think his name was. "Here we go." And the rope was cut, team members underneath caught the body, and slowly lowered to the floor. Where they removed the rope and then the cloth bag. What stared at us was a man. Or what used to be a man. His long grey hair obscured his face, but it was the cuts to the face that was the interesting thing. They looked as though they were carved, and almost like they were symbols. But they were covered with clotted blood, so it was difficult to make out. His eyes bulged, as they would with strangulation, making the face look small in comparison. His tongue hung, bloated just past his blue lips.

"Time of death..." Mary said taking the measure of the face colour and length of time hanging to kill a person. "Seven pm."

That hadn't been long, but then strangling someone by hanging wouldn't have taken long.

"Was there anything else?" I asked, knowing the autopsy results would show anything that we needed.

"Yes, now that you mention it, we found a rat."

"A rat? Why a rat?" Jeffries puzzledly asked.

"Well, it was the way the rat was killed. Not an ordinary death." Mary led us away from the body, so her team could get it, the rope and the bag taken back to the station. And led us to a little way away near the corner of the room. There a rat lay gutted.

"Ugh!" I said. "Why gut a rat here?"

"I don't know but thought it worth a mention. This clearly was before the victim was hung by the clotted blood. But the fact the time was taken to gut this poor creature is odd."

"Hmm." I pondered. "I wonder what that means."

"It means they found a source of entertainment while waiting." Jeffries said with a hint of salt. "Let's go Ma'am. We'll see you back at the station Mary. God, I hate heights." He moaned as we climbed back down the stairs.

On our return to the station, we did some hunting of our own. The ID had confirmed that it was Lucien Dogra. We tried to find out where he bunked for the nights, especially the ones that had nowhere else to go.

There were very little communities set up by those who did sleep rough. Most of the time, they bunked into doorways where they were sheltered and can be dry. Communities haven't been seen since the Hooverville in America. Now many feared to share a space, in case of theft or like this murder.

Luckily there was a small community in the warehouse near Mitre Square, that had taken root after the murders. It was as though having the police patrol was a safety net for them, and they took to it like ducks to water. An opportunity for safety free from harm and a place to sleep. One good thing came from those murders. A community.

Jeffries and I made our way there before they all slept for the night.

Jeffries yawned the whole way. He hadn't been sleeping well, Ann had been ill for the last two weeks and he was having to work and look after the children at night, the daytime Ann's mother was able to help. Jeffries didn't want special treatment, but I had offered some time off. He refused. Stubborn bull that he was.

The community was exactly as I had imagined. Dustbins being used as fire pits, pieces of driftwood used as poles to hold up large pieces of waterproof fabric like a makeshift tent. Bedding thrown underneath to ease the pain of sleeping on hard earth or on pavements. Violent coughing met us from all directions from each of the little tents. We saw eyes watching us, but no-one spoke. So I stopped dead in my tracks calling out. "I am D.I Abberline, don't worry we aren't here to tell you to leave, we want to know anyone who was close to Lucien Dogra! This is Sergeant Jeffries. We just want to talk!"

Coughs and feet shuffling met my words.

"Good luck with that," Came a grumble from nearby. "Everyone hated the bastard." He coughed. "He wasn't well liked around here."

"Why was that?" I crouched down, so I was in front of the tent.

"Well, he was a wrong un, you see."

"What do you mean by wrong un?" I asked.

"He used to mutter to himself a lot, talked about the conspiracies of Whitechapel. Said that the gates of hell had been opened and no one could close them while they were open. It wakes a person that does. Sleep is little and we takes it as we can." The man coughed again. I felt in my pocket, I had a couple of cough sweets, and I swore I would buy packets and distribute them here.

"Here. Take these." I offered the sweets. "They'll ease that cough of yours."

"That's kind that, not many folks would offer to help us." The man shakily took the sweets. "Your nice, I likes that."

I smiled. "Doing my duty as a policewoman."

The man peered at me again. "Say ain't you the copper that caught the Ripper?"

"That's me." I said, still smiling.

The man beamed a toothy smile. "You lady are a legend round here. We tip our hats to you for making the streets safer."

I nodded.

"Anything we can do to help, you lets us know." The man said, popping a sweet into his mouth and I could see the relief in his eyes when he looked at me next.

"Well there is something." I said, shifting on my feet. "We found Lucien today."

"What the fool do now?"

"He's dead, I am afraid." I whispered. The shock on his face showed.

"Dead? Jesus." He crossed himself. "I didn't like the fool but wouldn't wish death on a person." He paused. "Can I ask how?"

"He was hung." I replied patting the poor man's hand. "It would have been painful, its why we are here. We wanted to know where he slept or anyone that was close to him."

"No-one was, but oh. He slept in the blue shift there." He pointed a little away from his little house. "He lived there." He began to cry slightly. I offered a tissue.

"That's ok, we are doing are best to find out who did this and get them. You are safe that I promise." I said, patting his hand before standing.

"Thanks Ma'am." The man said before blowing his nose like a trumpet.

I waved Jeffries over to the hut that had been indicated.

"Your too soft." Jeffries scoffed.

"Well, wouldn't have got far if I was a hard rock." I laughed.

"True," We looked around the hut. There were a few possessions, very limited. There were the usual things you would stereotype with a member of this community, such as the bed rolls, the sleeping bag, the pillow, but in a little niche there were personal artefacts. A picture frame, some empty bottles, some of which had been decorated with lights, so they worked as a bedside table light. The picture frame was quite dusty, like it hadn't been looked at in a while, and so were the other empty bottle. Some batteries sat on the side as if the person was going to come back and use them. Most of the items in the little house looked that way. But we knew that would never be the case. I pulled on a glove, realising the sadness of it all and began searching. Jeffries was already a step ahead, he had been pulling things out to look for the reason as to why someone would kill this man, who had seemingly done nothing but mumble, to anyone.

I opened a little box that sat almost under the pillow and looked at the trinkets within. A ring, a bag full of herb, a whiff of which I got almost immediately. It was lavender. Amongst that, there was also a hand-made doll, made from wool. I recognised that. People made those- that was a worry doll.

As I moved the worry doll, it came apart, inside was a little picture and another item, but it was hard to make out. I grabbed a small evidence bag and placed the worry doll with its items inside. It was worth looking into. Out of the corner of my eye I saw Jeffries do the same.

Something in this little house had made Lucien a target for a killer. We were going to find out what that was. Then we could find this killer.

Chapter 12

We returned to the station, mainly to get what was in our evidence bags examined, but also to see how the rest of the team had gotten on.

It was a sad case, mostly because we all knew someone who had fallen on hard times like Lucien and we sympathised with them. Now seeing someone dead, because he was seen maybe as an easy target or as a leech on resources in these times, was a hard blow to all of us. As it could have been any of us.

Amy and Johnathon were working hard, cross examining everything about the building Lucien had been found in, they were also looking into the man's background. They were a good team, and we paired them together often. They were a little like Jeffries and I, a mismatched pair but one that worked well together. There would be a time when Jeffries wouldn't be there, due to retirement, but I honestly didn't expect that anytime soon. He was older than I was, but certainly didn't look or act like it.

Jack and Max were also working hard, looking into how he had been killed, I noticed with delight that they were on the phone with Barnett. Barnett had become a great resource, and should he have wished it, he would have been welcome on the team. No questions would have been asked.

They all were writing things on the whiteboard and Jeffries and I inspected it. A mind- map, labelled all the reasons why that warehouse was used. It's location. It's old use. Another mind- map labelled all the reasons of death. Some of which we had found out by visiting the community, so I circled them. Some of this job was a waiting game, and mainly to do with testing and the results.

It was tough for all of us.

When the news from the evidence bags came in, Jeffries and I were discussing our next move.

I wanted to go back to that warehouse again. Jeffries was against it, due to the heights. I wanted to look around and see if there was anything outside that could give any clues, Jeffries protested, saying that the crew would have already done that. I got more and more frustrated. It was only rechecking our steps, going over something in case something had been missed, he was putting obstacles in place.

"Ma'am, your results are back." Max popped his read around the corner of the door frame, and not a moment too soon. I was about ready to scream in frustration at Jeffries. Max disappeared to get back to what he and Johnathon would be doing, leaving Amy and Jack in the station, in case someone phoned in.

We went down to the laboratory, next to the morgue.

My feet felt like lead. I hated this part of the job, was there anything in the clues we had found or not.

But it turns out there was.

In my evidence bag, the results from the worry doll was that there was something stitched into the centre, another pack of herbs. These were tested and came back as mug wort. An ingredient used in herbal remedies. In Jeffries, there had been results of other herbs. Some had been sage, rosemary and thyme.

What did we have on our hands? This seemed to in the realm of Wicca. Not understanding this, I asked Barnett.

"Hey Joe,"

"D.I Abberline." He said, with a small smile. "Your team have already been in contact."

"I know. But I wanted to ask you something. What do you know about Wicca?"

"Wicca? That's a very strange request. But isn't it a form of religion?" He said. He was obviously on his computer as I heard the keys clack. "Wicca is a harmonious and balanced way of life, which promotes oneness and all that exists."

"Do you know anything about it?" I teased.

"No, I will admit I know nothing about Wicca. Witchcraft in the past however I do. And from what the others have told me, it sounds like someone is constructing a witch hunt. Those who followed Wicca used to be persecuted as a witch." He rustled some papers beside him. "The closest I have is in 1863, a man was drowned in a pond in Essex, in 1612, the Pendle Witches were hung, mainly hunted through Matthew Hopkins, the Witchfinder General."

"Give me a brief run down of the cases." I questioned, note pad at the ready.

"The man who was drowned there is no written information, but it is likely he was thought to be a witch, thrown into the pond to see whether he would sink or swim and when he drowned, they realised he wasn't a witch. The Pendle Witches were in Lancashire, twelve people were accused as being witches, one was not found guilty, two main families were the result of the accusations, rivals if you were. Village healers who used herbs and ancient remedies much like Wicca, basically one of the family members on the rival side asked one another family member of the rivals for something and when he refused this woman cursed him and he became stricken. They accused her of being a witch, along with many of her family over the course of months and years. They were hung due to being witches."

"Hung? So, hung by the neck until death?" I asked, pausing in my notetaking. It sounded familiar.

"Yes. If you were a witch you were said to have Devil Marks, such as a wart, mole or some strange marking that the devil had marked you with to suckle imps, familiars etc. And Matthew Hopkins was a firm believer if you possessed on of the above on your body, that singled you out as a witch." Barnett paused. "Ludicrous, as many innocent people were hung, burnt, pressed."

"Pressed?"

"Stones were placed on the person's chest and more weight was continuously added until death or the witch confessed or named another."

"Ouch."

"Very much so. It was a case in America, a man named Giles Corey during the famous Salem Witch Trials in 1692, he begged for more weight and died, being pressed to death, his innards suffocating under the weight."

I paused. The hanging was similar, so did we have a witch hunt on our hands?

"So, how would someone be classed as a witch?" I asked.

"Well if you had a devil's mark, were an independent woman without a husband in those days, had a surprising amount of wealth or were poor, didn't know your prayers, had a cat, bat or a toad, a dog in some cases, mainly if you were a female, if you had one or more female friends, that was classed as having a coven, if you had had an argument with one or more of your female friends, or with anyone else for that matter, you were very old, very young or under an influence of someone who is old, you are a healer, you are married and have none to few children. The lists were endless." Barnett concluded.

"What about if you exhibited strange behaviour?" Thinking of what the poor man who had told me about Lucien had said.

"Yes, very much so. If you lived near someone and the couple had trouble conceiving, you must have cursed them. It could be if milk or anything has soured in your possession, if you had sex out of wedlock, predicting the identity of a future spouse, broken a rule in the Bible and thus entered into a pact with the devil. Mags, this was all happening. The main reason that the Salem Witch trials happened or any of the trials was disputes, neighbours clamouring for land and ergot poisoning, causing hallucinations." Barnett pressed. "It has nothing to do scientifically in the existence of the devil, my Christian parents would roll in their graves, but it has to do with the surroundings and the environment."

I thought on this.

"Thanks Joe, that was helpful." Thoughts beginning to move through my mind, connecting with what had been said, what we had seen.

"I hope so and Mags?"

"Hmm?" I was thinking hard.

"There's no such thing as witchcraft." Barnett said as we hung up.

The fact that Lucien's behaviour had seemed strange, the fact that we had found herbs in his possession, linked to two of the potential signs of being a witch, many of the others had routes down the scientific as Barnett had said. What would the autopsy results show?

In fact, it showed a lot.

Standing infront of the body, we saw, another link. He had a birthmark and a mole on his shoulder. Someone who was playing the part of a Witchfinder General, had obviously seen these at some point before his death and looked at Lucien being a witch because of this. Plus, the herbs, plus the strange behaviour= a witch. It was as Barnett said, ludicrous. But if you were someone who truly believed in those things...that was the concerning thing. It could cause many people to die, over something that could a mental illness. And it clearly was, something that was purely in the mind. Poisoning? Or some form mental illness? It could have been one or the other. We had to catch the one doing this, before someone else got hurt.

Chapter 13

Someone else did get hurt.

They got hurt to the point that they had been branded, unlike the first person and then they were drowned. Drowned in their own bathtub.

The poor person who ended up being a victim of this crazed killer, was a poor middle aged woman, who lived on her own with her four cats, all black as pitch, and she had been only a member of a small knitting circle, who we suspected could be next on the killers list. Only because they had known this unfortunate.

They had plainclothes policemen keeping an eye on their houses. That was something the Chief had insisted on. I had taken the report, telling him that we could potentially have multiple victims again, like the Ripper if he didn't back me up. He didn't like it but had done so.

The poor unfortunate woman was Lucy Hale. And like the first victim, had a mark on her shoulder, she had been branded with what seemed to be a homemade 'w' poker. And tortured, when the killer had received no information, he had tied her to a chair while he prepared her death. All of this we saw in the report, she had rope burns on her wrists, legs and across her chest. Then in her lungs we found saltwater. To prolong her suffering, Mary had explained. She would have felt like she was burning from the inside out, along with the salt causing her burns to cause more pain.

This was gaining momentum. He was getting more and more extreme. He was determined to find the witch who had caused him pain, clearly, what pain we had not figured that out yet.

He was, either suffering from poisoning causing hallucinations, or he suffered from mental illness that was causing these hallucinations. Either way he needed to be stopped, so he could receive treatment for either. We would not lock him away without first treating the cause before we gave him a trial. Unfair to the justice system to try someone without baring in mind their mental state and capacity, that was against the law of course.

Something had to contribute to this. We were stumped. He was leaving behind no clues to his identity, not even a finger. It was silly to hope for a finger as a lead to who this person was. But that was the state of our team, there had been no hair or anything that had been left on the scenes. Not even a hair or a finger. Again, we had a ghost on our hands, but hopefully not a real ghost because that would be foolish.

We were going back over the details over the two murders, trying to see if the two victims had met one another recently. And we found something.

Lucien had encountered Lucy Hale, she had served him food at the food bank, and they had similar interests. She liked conspiracies and so did he, they had sat and chatted about his most recent one. And that was where it was similar. So, someone had to have seen the two talking, and that was our link between the two victims. But that someone, we still had no idea who it was. The only option we had to ask the food bank for a list of people, for that date that we suspected, and see what names there were. That way then we could at least follow it up with a house visit. And then we could look around for any sign of illness or potential poisons.

But we had no such luck, whoever they were they had either written down a non de plume or had not written their name down.

We were stuck, we had to hope, which we didn't like doing, that he would strike again and that this time he would be foolish to leave behind a clueor make a mistake. We had exhausted all other options.

And to our surprise that happened, as we arrived on the scene, this person, was burnt at a makeshift stake, in the bottom of her garden. Clearly the previous two witnesses had named the ones that we had seen. This poor victim, she was burnt beyond recognition. But we had hit some luck. This victim had written a note of someone that she would accuse and had swallowed it. Mary had discovered the paper in the stomach in the autopsy. We knew who the next victim would be. We were a step ahead like we had been with the Ripper. Finally!

The poor woman who had been burnt at the stake had been Arabella Henderson. Another lonely woman who shared a home with her sister. Her sister had been out of the country, visiting a relative in Australia. Luckily really or we would have had two murders at once. The most we had, had since the Ripper murders.

When the phone call came in that we had found the next victim, his name was Robert Anderson and that he was willing to work with us in order to stop this murderer, it was like music to our ears. We were getting somewhere. This soon to be victim, in the eyes of the murderer, this supposed witch had known all three of the other victims, he had worked on the gardens of Arabella, Lucy and helped feed Lucien at the food bank. He was twenty-seven.

He walked to work the following day, I was following, undercover of course, Jeffries hadn't liked it, but we had compromised, if no one looked suspicious then he would do the following day, and so forth. We would work in twos. Someone would be nearby, while the other worked undercover. I had made myself look like a homeless person, dirtied my hair, face and wore tattered clothing, that was stained with dust, water and sweat. I hated wearing it, but all in the cause for catching a killer.

I sat in there, eating my meal and eyes roving over everyone that walked in and worked there. No-one suspicious yet.

Then I saw him. He had been eyeing Robert with an almost eagle eye. An eye that was suspicious, one that was checking him over, looking for something. And he seemed to have found it. A tattoo. Now Robert had showed us all his tattoos when he had come into the station, the tattoo in question was of the runes iar-ia, feoh-f, and kalc-kk. Which meant serpent, wealth and chalice. I had researched them, long after he left. I had even drawn in pen on my hand, a few myself. Hoping to catch Robert's attention that it was me, and that if Robert saw them, he could name my alias as a witch and we would be able to get the killer. Jeffries had disagreed with me putting myself at risk. But my argument was that Jeffries would be able to surprise him, along with the other members of our team, like he had before to get the killer before he hurt me. Jeffries pride was inflated a little. It showed how much trust I placed in my team. And I am sure it showed.

Robert had seen my inked tattoos, looked at my face, given me a nod and carried on. He had also done the same with the killer. Took a good look. That way, it was easier to make a note of the person who was to kill him. I took a picture in my head as well. I would never forget that face though, the malice in the eyes was something that I had never seen before. Even with the Ripper.

The killer joined me on my table, it was almost concerning. I made sure to flash my hands in his direction and made sure to say goodbye to Robert, forging the connections. Jeffries met me a little way down the road from the foodbank, with a change of clothes.

"He was there." I breathed as soon as I had changed in an alleyway, slipped into the car. "He saw me, and he saw Robert."

"Hmm." Jeffries grunted.

"Sorry Bill, but if it means we can catch him then all the better for us, right?"

"Yeah, I suppose." He grunted again. "Just don't like using you as bait."

I shrugged. It would be worth it in the long run, I knew it.

Chapter 14

We followed Robert home that night. I had a feeling the killer would strike that night. He would not risk his prey getting away from him, he had sight of the two witches, and he would need to make them pay. For whatever they had done to him. We would find out when we caught him.

On the stakeout, we had a coffee, some takeaway food that Max had dropped off on his way around the corner, where the rest of our team were laying in wait.

When the shadow crossed the street diagonally across from us, we shifted. Getting low in our seats until he had passed, then quietly got out of the car. We silently followed. Jeffries texted the others letting them know we were on the move.

The killer walked straight up to the door, knocked and waited for someone to open the door. It was lucky we knew which floor that Robert lived on, and we were able to move as soon as the door was about to close, a hand stopped it from closing, mine. Of course, we then had to climb the stairs as quietly as possible to reach Robert's floor. Then we hung on the stairs until we heard the killer knock.

Robert answered the door, letting the killer in, why we were unsure. But he made sure to leave the door open for us as well, once the killer had entered, we moved. We hid around the corner by the door.

The sound of a scuffle, Robert crying out and we moved, I shot a bullet towards the killer and they jumped, literally. The threw themselves towards the window. But Jeffries shot another bullet before he reached it. The killer knelt on the floor. Hands were raised and he was mumbling.

"They deserved it, they did this." Over and over.

We arrested him there and then.

All was good in a night's work. We took him to the nearest hospital and got the bullet wounds looked at, we had aimed to hinder not kill. They cleaned him up, while he was still handcuffed. I also asked them to take a sample of his blood. The killer was Lloyd Walker. A patient who had Creutzfeldt-Jakob disease, in the stage of the Heidenhain variant. That caused his hallucinations and he hadn't been taking his medications.

We made sure he was secure in another hospital who would make sure that he would take his medications, making sure to write up in the report that he had a disease that played with his memory, changed his personality, changed the fact that the hallucinations he was having, was all to do with a witch cursing him with this disease that changed him. I couldn't help but feel that it was too easy to capture him, like underneath all the pain and the hallucinations he wanted help, but he had been too far in to stop. Like something had been compelling him through those hallucinations. I also believed that this wouldn't be the last case that we saw like this. I was an Abberline after all, I had this feeling multiple times over before each of our last cases. And it had turned out right.

My gut was telling me there was a worse case to follow this. But why were they happening? Again, my thoughts went to the Gates of Hell. What if it was true? And that was why all these cases were happening?

Again, my rational mind pushed these aside and I carried on writing the reports, giving my team some much needed time off. They went one at a time, we still needed a team in case.

It was while Jack would be off.

It was while Max would then clock out.

Then Johnathon.

Something would happen. Something would happen when it was just me and Amy, that I knew to be true. Jeffries was off, spending some much-needed time with his family when our last case together would happen.

It was a Saturday night, Amy and I were the only ones in our team's room, everyone else being off duty when Amy hovered in my doorway. It was late.

"Mags Ma'am?" She asked hesitantly. "Do you hear that?"

I looked at her, she was white as a sheet. "Hear what Amy?"

"The buzzing and the drip of a tap." She said. "I went to the bathrooms along this corridor, none of them are dripping. And I have hunted for the buzzing sound but there is nothing in there." She pointed.

I got up and stood where she was. There was a slight buzzing noise and a very faint dripping sound. Like water hitting a pipe. "I hear it now," I replied. "It's probably from one of the bathrooms upstairs. And maybe a lone insect got in and it's trying to get out."

"Mags, I went upstairs. No taps are even running up there, and the insect, I have hunted for that and I can see nothing." Amy's hands were shaking. "I am worried its in my head."

I listened again and didn't hear anything. "Maybe it was, we have been on some tough cases lately." I replied gently, the last thing she needed to hear was that she was crazy. "I hear things too when I have been stressed. I hear water running where there is none, and slightest noises sound magnified. Maybe someone has found the running tap and turned it off, and the insect has been let out now." I suggested. Amy shrugged; I could tell she didn't believe me.

"Maybe." Was all she said, "Do you mind if I take a quick break?" She asked.

"Of course." I glanced at my watch. "I am going to step outside for a cigarette if you would like to join me?"

"That would be nice." Amy smiled.

"Grab your coat, it's cold out." I said smiling in return. I grabbed my cigarettes, lighter and locked the door as we made our way outside, it was a force of habit now. Making sure our room was locked before leaving the building. After the trashed room, we were taking multiple precautions. Outside in the cold crisp air, we stood, our breaths puffing out into small clouds.

"Mags, would you mind if I have one?" Amy asked tentatively. I never knew she smoked, but if it took her mind of what was happening inside...

"Sure," I held out a cigarette and a lighter to her. She took it gratefully. Sparked up, and handed back the lighter, taking a deep inhale.

"Thanks, and Mags, I am sorry about what went on in there." She apologised.

"Nothing to apologise for Amy." I said and in companionable silence we smoked, seeing the smoke and our breaths become clouds that twisted and turned in the air, making incomprehensible shapes.

Amy seemed calmer now. Less white. She had a touch of pink in her cheeks, but that was from the crisp and frigid air. We finished our cigarettes, stumping them out before we headed back inside, rubbing our hands together to warm them up.

That was when I noticed her.

An old woman, standing, just staring at the precinct. She had a distinct look, heavy lidded face, dark eyes hidden beneath a wide brimmed hat. She was dressed in a dark skirt, blouse, with a thick coat over the blouse, and heeled Mary Jane shoes. I thought it odd, she looked out of place almost. And then I blinked, and she had walked away, not even giving the precinct a second glance.

I furrowed my brow. Surely, she had to be cold, despite the thick coat. A skirt in this weather? She had to be freezing, it did seem like an odd choice of clothes for the time of year, but perhaps she had dementia. That would explain it! Shaking my head, I walked back into the warm enveloping air of the station. I sighed.

When we wanted to stay busy, we had plenty of time on our hands and when we never had enough time, we always wanted to slow time down. This was one of those times. Making sure reports were written well from all the cases was one of the ways I kept busy. Amy, on the other hand was sterilising the place. She wanted to make sure no-one came back and sent colds and flus around the room. She was a little bit OCD, but we loved her for that. She kept us healthy. So, we never complained about it. Instead of sitting in my office, I brought the files and sat at Jeffries desk, she had already cleaned there, so I made sure not to mess it up too much. I think Amy appreciated the company. Before long she had finished, sat at her desk and began to look up some people for me for one of the cases. I needed to check the name, but Jeffries had locked his computer, as expected and I didn't know the password.

That was when we heard it. A dripping sound. Amy startled by the noise, jumped. I too jumped. Where was that noise coming from? It sounded as though it was over our heads... but there was nothing there? No bathroom or kitchen, so where was the dripping coming from?

Then it stopped. The lights flickered and Amy and I looked at each other. This was a coincidence. Surely?

When Jack came back from his leave, Amy couldn't wait to leave. Between us, we had been harassed with the dripping noise and the buzzing. We found no logical explanation but didn't want to venture into the unexplained. I couldn't leave until Jeffries came back. He would not be due back for some time, so I had to stay in case of a case.

Luckily Jack and eventually Max, returned, Johnathon had gone away to another country, he had transferred out. We had been sorry to see him leave but wished him luck on his new adventure. At least I had back up. But the sounds did not return, at least that's what I had thought.

They returned one night. The lights flickered and it made Jack's head shoot up. I carried on the only acknowledgement was my shaking hands. This time they did go out altogether. It was a manner of seconds, but it felt longer, in the dark you were more vulnerable, man or woman. I was never afraid of the dark but rather those that hid in it.

"Mags? Are you alright Ma'am?" Jack's voice pierced through the gloom.

"Mags?" Max asked.

"I'm fine. See if you can find some candles when they come back on. This happened a few nights ago." I hoped I sounded nonchalant. But maybe my voice quivered. I was unsure.

"How?"

"We aren't sure, an investigation over the building showed no signs of interference, no water dripping from anywhere, it must just be the old building." I shrugged though neither could see.

And then the lights came back on.

I blinked and thanked whatever deity there was for bringing it back silently.

"There should be some candles under Amy's desk." I said, "We used those the second time the lights flickered out."

"What's causing this though?" Max questioned.

"Must be the power companies." I shrugged. "This old building has had a lot of new electricity since my ancestor worked here. Some of the cables may have become lose or wires have become old."

On the inside I was thinking otherwise.

Chapter 15

The following weeks were tough on all of us. The dripping noises continued; the flickering lights also carried on as well. The whole experience had shot our nerves. Although it still was unexplained.

Jeffries returned from his leave, looking more refreshed than ever.

I was about to head off on mine when the call came in.

"There's been a body found in the cemetery. Not a usual body though."

I sighed, never being able to leave until this case was now solved. Such was the rule and the life of a police officer.

I grabbed my coat, thinking that Christmas was around the corner, why did this have to happen before Christmas. Someone will have lost their loved one, and who were the ones who had to tell them? Us.

We reached the cemetery. It was strangely not connected to St Patrick's which I found reassuring; I didn't know if I could ever stand in that cemetery again. Manor Park Cemetery. That's where this body was found. The person who had found the body had been on their way home from work, stumbling through the cemetery on the way, they tripped and landed feet away from the girl's body. And it was a very young girl. Looking down on her I guessed that her age was in the teenage sector. She still hadn't developed fully into a mature woman, and she lay on her back, eyes glassy and unfocused, her mouth was open in a silent scream. Her throat was cut, blood staining the top and hoodie that she wore. There were lesions around her mouth that suggested she had been gagged, before her throat was cut, around the throat above the incision, were finger marks, so not only had she been gagged, she had been strangled and had her throat cut. Mary was taking all the necessary photographs, she seemed disturbed by this. From what I gathered; Mary had a teenage daughter at home. Her hands were shaking slightly, no doubt thinking about her daughter as she studied this poor soul in front of us. When she came over however, her voice was strong, and her hands didn't shake.

"She has been strangled, gagged and also I am afraid to say raped."

I was horror-struck. All those things, perhaps all at once. As a woman, just one of those assaults was enough but to have multiples, it was unthinkable.

Mary glanced at my expression, that I was fighting to keep under control.

"Yes, all at once or the rape perhaps as she was being strangled and gagged, we won't know more until we have tested the body for any DNA left behind." She shook her head sadly. "The poor parents."

"Do we know her name?" Jeffries asked. I heard the hoarseness in his voice, the violence against this young girl surpassed a lot of the murders we had already seen, mainly because it was against a young girl, someone's daughter.

"Elizabeth Bedford." Mary said, pointing at her rucksack that lay hidden behind a gravestone. "We found books from school and a letter in the bag there."

Her poor parents. Not only would they have to deal with the fact their child had been killed but raped and suffered so much. It was enough to induce nausea. I knew, I could feel the bile in my throat.

"Do we know where they live from the letter?" I asked, forcing the bile down to my stomach.

"Mum lives up the road, Dad, well he lives in another part of the country." Mary said. "There were two letters, clearly she didn't want mum and dad to read them."

"A lot of trouble then." I said simply. I sighed. Time to head off to the mother's house, to tell her, her daughter was found dead tonight.

Jeffries and I headed to the home. It was in one of the 'slum' areas of Whitechapel, as Mary said around the corner from the cemetery. I knocked on the door to the number from the letter.

A woman answered. She was dressed in her dressing gown, a cup of tea in her hand, as if she had been expecting her daughter. She sighed. "What has she done this time?"

"I am sorry to say she hasn't done anything." I said, gesturing to the cup of tea I continued. "May we come in and you may want to put your drink on the table."

She let us, a puzzled expression on her face. As she took us into the living room, I spotted toys associated with a baby. So poor Elizabeth had been a big sister. The mother took a seat, placing her drink on the coffee table and gestured for us both to sit. "I am D.I Abberline and this is Sergeant Jeffries." I began. "We found your daughter tonight in Manor Park Cemetery. I am sorry to be the one to have to tell you this, but your daughter has been killed."

The poor woman, her hands went to her mouth, her eyes widening in shock, she looked as though she was about to faint. That was why I had suggested to sit down. Her face had lost all colour and she looked as though she was going to burst into tears.

"I'm sorry?" She whispered in disbelief. "Did you say Lizzie had been killed?"

I nodded. The woman burst into tears. I went over and patted her on the shoulder as she bawled her eyes out for her eldest child.

"Is there anyone else in this house that we could ask to help you in this devastating time?" Jeffries asked.

"No, my husband-Lizzie's stepfather, he's at work and won't be back until midnight. I was expecting Lizzie to come home after she had been at a friend's. She said she would help me with Miles, her baby brother."

The woman said in between tears. "Her father- Oh god her father! He needs to know."

"We can call him for you if you like?" I said softly. The woman shook her head.

"It should come from me. But you are welcome to talk to him afterwards, I know he would want to know everything. Same with her stepfather, he will want to know everything." She sobbed. I continued to pat her on the shoulders. This was the one thing about this job I hated, more than the puzzles, the grieving parents and loved ones.

"Maybe you should ring your husband." Jeffries suggested. "See if he can come home earlier."

She nodded. Her hands shook reaching for her mobile on the table. As she grabbed it, she fumbled with trying to unlock it. I offered to help her, but she shook her head. She dialled the number for her husband, we waited for him to pick up.

"Hi John, no it's me. Listen, any chance you can come home..." Her voice trembled. "Lizzie's dead."

He seemed stunned but assured her he would be home as soon as he could.

She then rang her daughters' father. He burst into tears over the phone. We could hear the distraught sobs. When he had calmed down, he asked how.

The woman handed the phone over to Jeffries, considering how I was comforting her.

He explained how we had found his daughter and what that means, that we were testing the body for DNA for the one who had done this to her. He asked to speak to the mother again.

"I am coming down there, I want to say goodbye, at least I can help you and John." He said, she only said "Yes."

Jeffries asked if should put the kettle on because of the newsand have a nice cup of tea. She nodded offering us both one. I took her up on it, we were waiting now for the stepfather to return.

Jeffries came back with three cups of tea and we sat in consolidating silence, sobs occasionally being uttered by the mother.

"I know this is a really devastating time for you, but could we ask you some questions while we wait for your husband?" I asked.

She nodded. "What do you want to know?"

"You said she had been at a friend's, which friend?" I continued.

"Her friend Beth, Beth Howson." The mother replied. "She said she was going there to study. She had this big test coming up after Christmas and Beth wanted to help. Then she said she would be home to help me with Miles. When she didn't turn up, I rang her mobile but got no answer, thinking that she had just forgotten the time."

"Her friend live round here?" Jeffries asked kindly.

The mother nodded. "On the other side of the cemetery, she must have cut through thinking it would take her less time."

"Did you know Lizzie had been given a suspension from school for fighting?" I asked.

"Fighting? Our Lizzie? No." She seemed shocked.

"She had hidden the letter to you and her father in her backpack, which we found nearby to her tonight." I said. "The letter said she had been suspended for hitting someone because they had been teasing a friend."

"That probably would be Beth. Lizzie always stood up to bullies, she stood up for those who couldn't stand up for themselves." Her mother explained. "That makes more sense."

We noted that down in our notepads. Then a rattle at the door and in comes Lizzie's stepfather. He looked completely shocked and looked straight from his wife to us.

"Jackie, whats happened, you said on the phone that Lizzie was dead." His voice trembled.

"It's true John, come sit, these lovely police officers have told me what happened, but we were waiting for you so I wouldn't have to hear it twice."

"Mighty kind of you." John-the stepfather said, sitting beside his wife, who immediately clutched his hand.

"Your daughter was found in Manor Park Cemetery about over two hours ago. We had our forensics experts take the official look; she is also taking your daughters body to our morgue where we can see what the official cause of death. I am sorry to say that Elizabeth had been strangled, her throat cut, gagged and raped." I said. The mother's face dropped in horror and her hands went straight to her mouth, she looked as though she was going to throw up. The stepfather on the other hand, looked us dead in the eye and said.

"What?"

Now usually if someone is told that their daughter or stepdaughter is dead, there would be some sort of emotion, like her fathers had been. But to be told how the stepdaughter had died, and you utter merely one word, is a little odd.

But it could have been just how he dealt with the news. "We believe at this stage, that your daughter was walking through the cemetery, after your wife has told us, on the way back from her friends house, thinking she would get home quicker, and was attacked. At this stage we do not know whether she was gagged, then strangled and raped or whether she was gagged, strangled, had her throat cut and raped. We will know more after the autopsy and the testing for DNA so we can catch the person who did this." I said, looking him straight back in the eye. The mother then ran into the kitchen and we heard her retching into the sink, the stepfather blankly looked between the kitchen to us. "I know this is horrible, but could we ask you some questions?" I asked, "We want to make sure we have the full picture so we can investigate around the time of her death."

"Sure, I got nothing to hide though." Uh, huh, sure you didn't I thought.

"Where do you work?" Jeffries asked.

"Rohima, I stack shelves." He said simply. "I went to work at 5pm and was supposed to work until midnight."

"Is that a usual thing?" I asked.

"Yes. Usually Lizzie will do her own thing but help out her mother during that time. Jackie rang me when Lizzie didn't come home, so on my break I phoned her to remind her she was needed at home." He said. Listening for his wife.

"So, we have just told your wife that Lizzie had been suspended for fighting, did you know about that?" I asked again, I could see holes in his story. Things didn't add up.

"Yes, she was covered in bruises and cuts when she came home one day, didn't want me to tell her mum. So, I helped her by getting her some ice packs, some bandages and let her clean herself up." He said. Again, there was limited emotion. I was getting vibes from him and not the nice ones.

But I couldn't let on that I suspected him. He could run.

"And you didn't tell your wife?" Jeffries asked, I could see the pensive look on his face that indicated he was thinking along the same lines as I was.

"No, with the new baby, it's been stressful. She's had postpartum depression and has struggled. Lizzie had been helping, but its going to be harder now." His voice then broke. Before this he had been talking about Lizzie in the present, but now it had shifted to the past.

We had to check his alibi.

"Thank you." We stood, shook his hands, and called. "Thank you, we will be heading off now. Thank you for the tea, and we shall update you both soon with what we find. We are so sorry for your loss." Jeffries and I exited the house and I took a deep breath.

"Did you believe him Mags?" Jeffries asked when we had walked away from the house towards our car.

"Not one bit, the bit about working and the fact he changed from talking about her in the present and then changed. I don't know Bill it's fishy." I said.

"I agree." Jeffries said. "I will ring his work and see when he clocked in, and I will ask for CCTV as well."

I nodded. "Thank you."

"You should go on your leave, or you will never get any." He finished.

"I couldn't, not going to leave you all in the middle of this. As soon as this is over, I will leave straight away." I laughed.

Chapter 16

So far, the stepfather's alibi was correct. We went down another route, talking to some people who had been walking by the cemetery when they had seen Elizabeth walking through it, although it was dark, they said they saw her neon backpack in the darkness. They also said before she had walked through, they saw a man lurking in the graveyard, a tall man who wore dark clothes.

We had another lead, which was good. The DNA results came back. There was nothing on her, the killer had clearly even wiped his own semen away carefully, no hair, no fingernails nothing. It had been a long night, and it wasn't over yet.

I knew one thing. I needed a cigarette. I knew that for certain, after the hell of a night we had, had. So, leaving Jeffries in charge of handing out the assignments for the team, I stepped out. Even though I knew it would work, for some reason my lighter stopped working. I pulled a cigarette from my pack, tapped the lighter against my hand, before it emitted a spark and lit the cigarette, taking a deep drag. I closed my eyes. It had already been a long night. But the worst was yet to follow us.

Just before I went back in, I saw her again. That same woman but this time she had a young man with her. The young man he was dark skinned, had black hair, quite tall and well-built and he looked familiar in a way. The woman had changed too. She had gotten younger, if that was at all possible. For some strange reason I thought she was a different woman. But then I saw her eyes. The same dark eyes caught hold of mine. A shiver went down my spine, but I couldn't move away. I was frozen in place. Then the young man saw me too, his eyes were pitch black. Then he smiled. That smile sent terror and I felt as though I was no longer in control of my body, it refused to move. I screamed inside. Then as soon as it came, it was gone and I tore my eyes from the creepy pair and ran inside, panting as I stood outside the team room. I swore I hear maniacal laughter. But that must have been my overactive imagination.

It had been nearly a month since that night, and I had not seen that pair since.

And we had just been called to another murder.

This was another young girl, the same age as Elizabeth Bedford.

She had been found inside an onion sack in a cemetery, East London Cemetery.

This poor girl had also been strangled, raped and had her throat cut. Again, the same lifeless and glassy eyes, the same silent scream. It hurt to not only tell Elizabeth Bedford's parents again, but this time we had to tell another set of parents. This time I sent Amy and Jeffries; I could not go through that again. Instead I stood in the cemetery, watching Mary work, keeping out of her way mainly. But I was trying to work something out. Why these two young girls where before we were having women and men, what's changed?

What was the idea of having them placed in cemeteries, what was the point? And what were they trying to replicate? Barnett had no idea although he would do his research for us.

I had been doing my own research, I had been looking into whether there was a pattern with the murders, the main ones kept coming back to the Ripper murders, and that was when I realised that two of our murders, the more recent ones, were in cemeteries were Annie Chapman and Elizabeth Stride were entombed. Just like I had been taken to Mary Jane Kelly's with the head of the women who had been poisoned and dismembered. So that was three out of five confirmed Ripper murders. Looking at an old map of these murders they form lines. I then did research on lines in the UK, ley lines came up. It was almost identical, it just ran the opposite way, as no ley lines ran through Whitechapel, was someone trying to recreate one? The power of ritual I understood, but what was this ritual? That concerned me, and to what did this ritual do? What was the aim?

I knew I could never voice this to my team, they would laugh at me. Though with what had been happening, Barnett at least would understand where I was coming from, so I broached it one afternoon. I closed my office door and rang him.

"Joe, it's Mags. I have a really quick suspicion I want to run past you."

"Go for it Mags."

"Could this be a ritual, I have been doing some research, call it gut instinct, and most of the murders we have had so far, meaning there could be more. They form lines. Like ley lines."

"Someone has been busy." Barnett laughed. "It could be a potential thing. Let me see if I can start pinning these down. Perhaps you could come by and we can work on that together, as I assume you cannot take this to your team?"

I sighed. "No. They would laugh. That sounds like a good idea, at least then I would have someone to bounce ideas off."

"Very well, let me get all my materials together and I shall ring you when I am ready."

"Thanks Joe, that means a lot to me." I said, and Barnett promised to have it all soon and we hung up.

In the meantime, we had a job to do. And dejectedly, another murder occurred.

This one was unrelated to the ones that we had, had with the two young girls, although it was in another cemetery. This young woman was wearing a long maroon dress, with brown tights underneath, black buttoned boots that looked a little old fashioned but old fashion did come back into fashion for those younger than us, a cardigan over her shoulders. She was about five four in height, so a little shorter than me.

Beside her lay a small claypipe. Which was old fashioned as no one used those anymore. It was I would have imagined Sherlock Holmes with. Her skirt of the dress had been pulled up, blood was on her thigh, and on the abdomen, which had come from a zig-zagged cut that ran from her left breast down to her navel. She was found outside the City of London Cemetery and Crematorium. Another two of the Ripper's victims was also entombed here. We had hit five out five. There was a link there. Was this killer bringing us back to where we had started? I would only know when Barnett and I would meet and figure this out.

Not long after the murder, Barnett got into contact, and I headed there straight after work. I told Jeffries I was going to talk to Barnett at his place as there I could study data alongside him. And if we found anything then I would let the team know.

The scene I arrived to see a whiteboard in Barnett's living room with a huge map of Whitechapel, including the Ratcliffe Highway. He had already plotted some of the murders we had seen.

"That's impressive Joe." I said.

"Thank you I have been busy, while you've been out seeing the murders, I have been plotting the ones we knew about." He handed me a cup of coffee. I took it happily.

"Let's correspond with history as well Joe, there's something happening in Whitechapel, and I want to stop it."

Barnett smiled. "How did I know you were going to say that?" He laughed. He took post it notes writing the deaths of the Ripper victims on them and then placing them on the map, then he did the same with the poisoner, the Thames Torso killer and the Ratcliffe Highway murders.

It took us most of the afternoon with multiple coffees and in my case cigarettes outside.

There was a picture. There was. It looked as though someone was mimicking a ley line, ley lines were used to draw on significant power.

Someone was after that power, for what we weren't sure. That stumped Barnett.

"Who could want to amass that amount of power?" He asked.

"Who ever is behind all these murders." I said and then I told him about the strange couple I had seen and the oldy lady I had seen before. He seemed terrified when I told him how they had made me feel.

That was when I received another phone call.

"Mags, you need to get back here. There's been another one." I looked at my watch. "I'll be ten minutes to get back to the station, where is the murder?"

"Agar Grove."

"I'll meet you there." I hung up on Jeffries. I turned to Barnett. "Thanks for this Joe, and we'll meet up after I find out about this murder."

"Why don't I come with you? I can drop you there at least." Barnett suggested. "It seems like whoever is behind these is gaining momentum, like there is an urgent date he needs this done by."

I nodded. Barnett locked his house and we jumped into his car, making it to Agar Grove just before Jeffries.

"What happened?" I asked Jeffries as Barnett stood beside us, watching. Jeffries merely pointed to Barnett. "I was with him when I got the call, he wanted to come and see if he recognised it from any of his research."

Jeffries just nodded. "A runner ran this way on a whim and found the body. He called it in."

"You ok?" I asked. He seemed out of spirits.

"Yeah, just wish these would end." He sighed.

"Me too Bill."

We walked until we came to the body. Her throat was cut ear to ear. She held keys in her right hand. Almost as if she had just come home, ready to unlock her door. If we hadn't known any better, from the way she was lying, and with her eyes closed. We would say that she had merely fallen asleep on the doorstep. But that was without the throat being sliced open. Another young woman, another family, another death.

The killer or even the person behind these murders was gaining momentum. We had no leads; no suspects and it was starting to show. Barnett had said that the previous two murders sounded like ones that had occurred in Liverpool in the 1900's. This more recent one, he said sounded like a murder that happened in 1907, a prostitute called Emily Dimmock had been found her bed asleep by her partner her throat cut just like our victim. Pressure was starting to pile down on us from above. But we had nothing, no leads, we had no idea who had killed the two teenage girls, there was very limited information, even from the forensics. Our killers had been careful. We brought in the stepfather to one of the girls again and double checked his answers to what he had already given, we rechecked CCTV, we then found something. John Bedford had left his work at the time that we believed his stepdaughter had been killed, wearing a dark coat. He grew angry and threatened us. When he had been restrained, he then admitted to killing her. He admitted that he had, had sexual fantasies about her, only because of the way she had been dressing lately. And the fact that a new baby meant that he couldn't have her mother.

We locked him away when he then admitted to killing the second girl. Saying that she had been dressed provocatively and he needed to satisfy his urges, so he did. He didn't want to be linked to the murders because of the baby and his wife. When we told his wife, she burst into tears and disbelief shouting that "How could he? I married a liar, a paedophile!" and sobbed her heart out. Luckily, Elizabeth's father said he would stay and help her out during the time of grief with the baby and that she was welcome to come and live with him away from all this in Liverpool until she was back on her feet. She had gladly accepted his offer. My hunch and Jeffries had been right. But that didn't explain our latest murder, with no suspect. No way of knowing how this poor woman had been targeted. Or why she had been targeted.

Chapter 17

We were exhausted, we were brow beaten again. This was becoming a regular thing.

Barnett had been brought in as a researcher, on the team. The team welcomed him with open arms.

He helped us solve the murder of the young woman- Alice Reeves. That had been her name. She had been killed by a mugger, who had stolen her bag. We had found him after he had pawned a woman's gold necklace and arrested him there and then, when he admitted he did it.

It all seemed easy, too easy.

I had gone eventually onto my leave, and I didn't know what to do with myself. So, I sat mainly on my balcony, smoking cigarettes, breathing in the fresh air. Worrying mainly. Something big was around the corner. I could feel it. I was worrying about my team as well. Barnett said that it was probably nothing, but he would keep an eye on them for me. Jeffries was retiring after New Year's. He had told us after we had solved the Alice Reeves case. It had been hard for him, his wife Ann had been made redundant at the hospital that she worked at, because they couldn't justify her working there anymore. Luckily, she had managed to find a job at a care home, so she wasn't out of work. But that meant early morning shifts, where Jeffries was working at the station on our cases, he couldn't let his children be ushered off to school early, he wanted to be there for them, and the stress was beginning to get to him. He said he had, had enough of police work, so if he needed to, he would become self employed and he was in the middle of creating his own line of psychotherapy for those in the police force who needed someone to talk to about murders or scenes of horror that they may have witnessed. I was pleased to hear that he was thinking about retiring, I would be sad to see him leave. But we had to do what we had to do now, we had to think about our families.

When the time came for me to leave my home, when it wasn't for groceries, and head back to the precinct, I was ecstatic. I didn't do well with being told not to work, so I had been, just researching times of year that were good for performing rituals. And I found a lot. New Year's, Samhain- Halloween, these were good times of year to perform rituals and gain an enormous amount of power. Samhain would be more the preferable, and I had guessed that perhaps that would be the tine to be more aware.

Things at work had slowed.

It was a little worrying.

New Year's Eve was also quiet. Well, we had the usual complaints about noise, fireworks, partiers who were drunk and passed out on the streets, so we were able to complete those tasks reasonably well.

Soon came the time for Jeffries to retire. The whole team celebrated him, his work at the station and being their sergeant. He was an amazing man, he had a few tears in his eyes, that he hid quite quickly when he thought someone was watching. After work we went to the local pub and had a drink in celebration. He deserved it and I thanked him for being an amazing Sergeant, wished him well on the future adventure that he was going on and I saw him wipe a few tears away as I spoke but didn't call him out on them. He and I had butted heads quite frequently over the years, and I would miss him. We all would as a team.

Later that night, as many of the team decided to head to grab a kebab, before heading home, I saw Jeffries pull Barnett aside. They spoke quietly for some time, before they shook hands. Then Jeffries came over to me. "Thanks Mags. You have been a brilliant D.I and I am going to miss you." He shook my hand. "I am sorry about the beginning and many times when I questioned your judgement."

"What's a sergeant for?" I joked. Though I could feel the tears coming. I wasn't an emotional person, but Bill Jeffries had earned my loyalty, respect and a friendship. "It will be strange without you Bill."

"Ha, but you'll get on without me."

"Yes, but it won't be the same." I said, my throat closing because of the tears I wanted to cry.

"Now, you take care of yourself." Bill said. "I won't be around to do it for you."

"Stay in touch Bill." I laughed at his statement.

"You too Mags, you too." Then he left. I sat finishing my drink before leaving and heading home.

Months flew by, and over time it was getting easier to work without Bill. But it still stung on occasions when I went to call him, and I choked on the words.

The rest of the team were just as forlorn. Getting used to being without their sergeant was demanding and tough. They had to come directly to me, instead of asking him. Many of them will apply to the sergeant's position and I wished them well, knowing I would have no input in the decision that will be made. But I still encouraged them all to go for it. It would also mean that new members would join our small but tight-knit team. And we would have to have them get used to the way we worked, get them to hit the ground running as it wore.

Our new team members were Oliver and Lilly they became the youngest on the teams at twenty-three and twenty-five. Jack became the new sergeant at twenty-nine. I was happy for him, he was thrown into the deep end though without much training, in charge of the new recruits as it were. Luckily, he had Amy's and Max's trust and respect. Without it, and mine he was a sitting duck as the two new recruits didn't understand that he had seen much and had more authority than them. They constantly tested him. One day after letting him conquer it himself, I backed him up, saying if they didn't like then transfer, Jack's word was just like mine, it was an order either way and if they couldn't follow those orders then they were going to be transferred. Jack seemed happy I intervened, and they soon began to follow his orders.

More months passed. The team became a unit again. And we needed it just in time.

The missing persons team brought to our attention a string of people that had gone missing over the past months. They had been unable to find hide nor hair of them. They had disappeared.

What hope we had to find them when they couldn't I was unaware of, but Jack's optimism kept us going. He had seen what we had been previously up against, where the two new recruits hadn't although they had heard about it. And he knew we could crack this.

September rolled around and we had still had no luck finding the missing people. Barnett had been looking into history's missing people who had gone missing, though we had no leads on which to base his research. I was beginning to become worried. October was the next month, and with that came Halloween, All Hallows Eve, Samhain. We had to find these people before the ritual I believed was still going on, had met its completion. Whoever was clamouring for power would have that power soon, and then all Hell would break loose.

We searched like a team possessed.

We hunted down last known whereabouts, leading mainly to a club and a bar that all the missing people had ended up, but they had not seen them since. Suspects came and went as we went through the lists. Oliver and Lucy, well they were being introduced to this aspect that I had begun. When they had been told, I had been the one to catch the Ripper by being bait, they were shocked. That had been unexpected. The only option was to do that again.

I dyed my hair. I had become a red head. Ironic, considering in the movies Mary Jane Kelly had been a red head, where it was more than likely she had been a brunette. Considering the historical facts. Again, we had come full circle. I wandered through the cemeteries holding the women's remains, praying to whatever God there was, praying that I would not be one of the ones to go missing. I crossed myself at Mary Kelly's, Catherine Eddowes, Elizabeth Stride, Annie Chapman and Ann Nichols' graves hoping that the spirits of the women were with me as I made my way to the bar and club on separate consecutive nights.

Nothing. Nada. Zip.

I was dejected. I knew that somewhere there was a someone who knew where these people were. It was highly unlikely that these people were still alive, although most of the city believed otherwise. It was harsh to think that all those people were dead, but otherwise they would have been found. And it was blue to feel that they would never be found at this point.

There had to be one other place that they all visited before they disappeared. There had to be. Otherwise it made not a lick of sense.

A week later, we found out from Max and Oliver that there was a new pie place opened on Fleet Street. I was a bit dubious to try one, knowing the history of Fleet Street, but when Max brought one in for everyone and I tried one, I found it delicious.

There was something about the meat in the pie though. It had a taste that was unfamiliar, maybe a different type of beef or pork?

Either way it tasted agreeable.

Chapter 18

We had been hunting those poor missing people for a long time. It made zero sense. Where had they spent those last moments before they disappeared. It certainly wasn't the club or the bar. I had revisited those places, sticking around until closing time. Asked a few questions, throwing in names that had gone missing. The results were the same.

"Haven't seen them in a while."

Meanwhile, we had once a week a pie from that new meat pie place. It always tasted delicious.

It fuelled us enough to keep going, to keep looking into places those people visited. Still the same results.

"Haven't seen them in a while."

To go back and speak to their families, hoping they would have something for us to investigate.

They gave us the leads, but the leads weren't enough.

"Haven't seen them in a while."

The families were growing impatient, angry and frustrated. They wanted to know whether their son, daughter, wife, mother, father would be found and if they were dead, to be allowed to grieve, to be allowed to bury them.

Some of them had already opted to have a closed casket, due to the length of time that their family member had gone missing. Then they refused to give us any more information and closed doors in our faces.

I understood the frustration, the anger and the beginning to lose faith. The police force had been severely lacking in places. I felt frustrated, angry and refused to lose faith in my team, we were working hard. We were the ones hope was placed on, and we used that hope as a fuel, we carried on.

One night, I sat in my office, combing through reports, CCTV footage, and that's when I spotted her.

That same woman, the woman I had seen outside the police precinct, once on her own and once with that young man. She appeared on the footage a couple of times. Each time she was dressed differently but she was there. She was at the club; she was at the bar. She had even been in some of the places that the families had said their family member had been to before their disappearance.

I called Jack in. "Jack!" He came sprinting in. He had a smile on his face.

"Yes, Mags Ma'am?"

"Come and have a look at this." I held the photos and laid them out so he could see them all at once. "This woman has appeared in all the places our people have been in before they disappeared."

"That's Iris Rouse. She's the one who owns the pie place on Fleet Street." Jack said.

"Iris Rouse? Have we done anything to look into her?" I asked.

"No but I can get someone to look into her with me." Jack said, his smile had never faded.

"Thanks Jack."

"No problem Ma'am." He nodded at me, getting straight to work. I missed Jeffries, Jack was great, but I missed Jeffries. He and I knew what the other was thinking. He always had an idea what was going through my head as I was thinking. Jack still had so much to learn, but I knew he would get there, he just needed experience. And I was happy to give it to him.

And true to his word Jack did just that.

He found not a lot on Iris Rouse, but he came to me with a plan. He and Max would go and talk to her. He would then ask her about her pie business and ask her how long she had been in London. He then would come back with the information she had given him, compile a profile and tell the whole team, anything that comes out of it. I was impressed with the amount of detail that he had gone into. It showed that he wanted to do well at being a sergeant. I had agreed to the plan but added if they ran into any issues to get out of there as soon as possible, pretending they had been called to a job and coming straight back to the station. We could always send someone else if that would be the case. I could always go incognito. He had agreed. He said he would look up her hours of working on the way home tonight and feed back tomorrow morning, adding to his plan so that he and Max could work out a strategy.

I would also be doing my own research with Barnett's help.

It was a struggle, Jack and Max had left that morning for Fleet Street. The plan would be if we hadn't heard from them, one of the others would phone them, saying we had another murder. Barnett and I had begun our own research. He started in history while I started looking her up.

Nothing.

There was nothing on her before she had opened her pie shop. That was odd, usually there is a birth record, that is if she had been born in England. I investigated the avenue to other countries, but still the same information.

It was like before now, she never existed!

How could that even be possible?!

Barnett also came back with nothing, apart from some old pictures that depicted the same woman, but we thought that it was just an ancestor. Nothing mysterious about that.

It was alarming that we could find nothing on her.

But we chalked it up to her not being registered at birth, having a different name when she was born, though there was nothing on a name change on the system either.

This was all strange.

How could we find out about this woman when there was nothing about her? Did this mean she was involved in the disappearances? If so how?

Max and Jack appeared some time in the evening, both wearing puzzled looks on their faces. They told me that she had eluded to nothing from her past and that her meat pies were her grandmother's recipe. How could that be? There was no record of any Rouse's. Apparently, her mother's maiden name had been Routledge. But even so there was not anyone by the name Routledge in our files. Or any files for that matter.

Jack had felt like she knew why they were there, and deliberately kept changing the subject to the disappearances, wondering if we had found anything on those poor people. Jack had said that it was an open investigation and therefore couldn't discuss it. Apparently, she had chuckled. Max also admitted there was a strange smell in the air, one he couldn't quite place. And the air had been thick with cooking herbs and spices, which made it harder to distinguish.

We showed the two what Barnett and I had found; they came to the same conclusion as us. A relative, or ancestor with the same looks.

Meanwhile, Halloween was edging closer and closer.

Whoever was causing these disappearances, their ritual would soon be complete. And I knew that once it was, we would never be able to find murderers again, I knew it in my gut.

Chapter 19

Our hunt had come to a standstill.

Unrest followed from the public.

Like the Ripper we were hounded by people screaming at us, some even began throwing stones through windows of cars. They were arrested for that.

But it didn't put a damper on their abuse. It carried on, to the point where their words rang in my ears every night.

I lost sleep. I couldn't remember when I had, had a decent night's sleep. I awoke, from nightmarish figures hounding my dreams. I always awoke in a slick sweat, showered and always ended up on my balcony. Smoking and thinking.

Thinking and smoking.

No people had currently gone missing, and yet we were still trying to find them. To no avail.

It was a mystery how they had appeared and the fact that we had not found a hide or a hair of them.

It was odd.

On a whim I looked for people who had gone missing in history, in England, there were a few that had gone missing. But many of them had been found. We were talking people who went missing because of the Titanic, for the people who had gone missing before the ship had set sail, before that when a killer roamed the streets of Whitechapel, I had first hand experience of how that had felt, of people who had gone missing around that time. Thought to be a victim of said Ripper.

One lot of missing people did stand out to me, I had rung Barnett and asked him to do the similar research and see what he came out with and we would compare. If he found the same as me, then we could make a case and take it to the team, until then I thought a lot. Things connected in my head. A lot of things connected. The fact that the Ripper murders began to be copycatted, the Thames Torso Killer, the witch hunts, the poisoner Marquis De Sade/Isabella and the Basil pot. They were all happening as they had before, for a reason. Someone was controlling them, I hated to admit that something supernatural was occurring, hellish even, but it was the only thing that connected the murders. I suspected Iris Rouse and her strange companion from that day outside the station. On a second whim, armed with a glass of wine, I looked at photographs from the Ripper murders. There she was. Hidden in the background. The Thames Torso Killer- she was there also. And then I inspected the others and there she was. She was in all the photographs with every killer, she was there in the background. Sitting, standing, posed there as though she knew, a small smirking smile on her face as though she knew, where we were perplexed, she had a self-satisfied smirk that read 'I know, and you never will'.

I blew those images up, hoping that Barnett was likeminded as I was to see the connections. She had been there the whole time. We had missed her, and we had a good reason too, she faded well into the background. As if she were nothing but air. There was no excuse, evidence that she was involved, no matter her innocent looks now, there was something about Iris Rouse, that was not innocent, sinister and demonic.

As I looked at her pictures, the cold air rushed around me chilling me to my very bones. This had to be the right track, whoever that man was he was involved too, though I found no evidence that he had been involved from the beginning. The more recent murders and cases, he was there, loitering in doorways or on the corner of streets.

Somehow, they were behind this. All of it. It would be my job to find them and bring them to justice.

That was when we had another murder.

Had they sensed I had figured it out? Was this a ploy to get me off their back?

The morning of the murder had been dull, and no rain had been forecasted, such was the weather in England, until the heavens opened that was. The streets were dampened with silver rivers. The pubs, bars, restaurants had all been busy, packed tight from front to back with people seeking shelter from the piercing rain.

Our victim had clearly been in a fight before her death, her eyes were blackened, her ear had been cut, and something had been rammed into her abdomen and up into her from another angle, that I as a woman winced at. There were similarities between her and the Ripper murders, but it was different. Mary would tell us after she had done the autopsy that a blunt object had been thrust into her abdomen, a piece breaking off into the intestines, and a sharp, pointed stick had been shoved up into her reproductive system from her vagina. I knew I winced; it was shaped like a stake that one would use on a vampire. Mary winced when she showed us the stick and the item found in her intestines, it was the end of the jack knife, one uses to open boxes. Jack was astounded. The amount of force needed to do that would have been immense. Who were we looking for? A man or a being with immense strength to kill the woman like this.

She had no family left living, no-one to mourn her death. No lovers, boyfriends or girlfriends. She had been alone. Alone in life and alone in death. That was the saddening thing. No-one to mourn her or to remember her.

Was that all we were? Dust that no matter how we look at it, we die alone in the end?

We took her to the morgue, and I happened to glance around at the scene of the crime, and who should I see?

Those two!

One stood talking to one of my team, talking explicitly about what we should do. How she saw her walking with a young man, but it had been too dark to see him properly. And him leaning against a wall, near an alleyway. As if he was completely bored with the situation. I averted my eyes quickly, unless they saw me looking. I had my proof. They were involved. They were at the scene of the crime, or were they returning to see their outcomes.

Who knew but them?

On the return to the station, I gathered my team together, Barnett and I bringing information that we had compiled, as well as the information that Jack and Max had compiled. The rest of the team seemed shocked. And in complete disbelief.

Jack, being quiet for so long even added. "But there was something off about that place, just now I cannot put my finger on it."

"What did she say her ingredients were?" I asked Max.

"She didn't, just laughed like I had made a joke, so we changed the subject pretty quick."

Silence met his words.

"And the smell?" Barnett asked. "The unidentifiable smell that hung underneath herbs and spices?"

"I asked about that and she waved it off, saying it was the building." Jack added, his face reaching realisation. "Do you think she's putting people in those pies!" He exclaimed.

I was pretty sure all of us just about threw up.

One by one we eventually did. Amy started the chain reaction and it ended with me.

All into our bins. Or rushing to the gents or ladies. We all threw up the contents of our stomachs, realising we had eaten the very bodies we had been searching for, for over a month.

Halloween was soon going to be fast upon us. Mere days away. We didn't have long to come up with a cunning plan to catch her and make sure that nothing happened on Halloween.

Life got in the way.

Another murder.

And then another.

And then a third.

It was though they knew we knew. And were trying to throw us off, by sending more work our way.

The first murder was of an electrician, who had ended up in a butcher shop mere moments from the police station, the butcher in question had no idea how he had got there, and the CCTV showed the electrician walk to the door, went all fuzzy and showed the poor man dead.

He had family, a little girl and a baby boy back at home. Killed for no reason, that came clear. Organs had been missing, however. So, we assumed someone was harvesting those organs for a reason.

The second murder was a young woman, she had ended up on a pig farm. She also had organs missing, from what we had found of her. The pigs had gotten to her first. Her brother had found her in the sty and pulled her away before the pigs could finish the job. Apparently, like the first she had come home late, and just had not entered the home.

Family.

The third murder was the real puzzle, and I detested this one. A young woman; had been strangled with her own washing in her garden, mutilated, much like the Ripper, but it was not like the Ripper, her groin was ripped open, cuts on the back of her legs and back. It was nothing like we had seen, but apparently history had. It was like one found in

New York City. In that case no organs had been removed, save for one ovary, but in this case, organs had been removed.

Again, this young woman had a young child that relied on her, she was a single parent, killed while doing her housework while her child slept, we were alerted by someone looking out of their window and the child's cries. It was devastating, knowing that a young child had lost her mother, because someone decided her mother needed to die. She would grow up alone. In foster care if she was lucky, be adopted into a loving home. But that was rare in Whitechapel, it would be more likely that she would be taken out of London and moved elsewhere in the country.

These were murders, with no real suspect. But who did we find? The same two people, languishing in the pain and devastation that had been caused. By whom, we still had no idea, though they being at the root of it all was questionable.

Chapter 20

Halloween was literally, two nights away. We seemed busy, but in all actuality, we were stumped. We had no idea how we were going to get the couple to admit they were behind all the murders or how we were going to approach them. Jack, Max, Oliver, Barnett and Amy were completely against me being bait again. They knew this time I would not be so lucky.

That was when I got a call from Jeffries.

"D.I Abberline." I said, looking through a case file.

"Mags." I knew that voice.

"Bill! How are you?" I smiled for the first time in days.

"I'm alright you?" I could hear that in all fact he really wasn't ok.

"Been better, now what's up, this isn't a social call." I stated simply.

He sighed. "Mags, there's something odd with Fleet Street. I have been investigating and before you scold, it was for a client. A young man has taken residence in the topmost floor, no others have been interested in this place before, people have been entering his space and never coming out." I dropped my pen in surprise.

"How?" I sat up a bit straighter, had Bill succeeded where we hadn't?

"I've been sitting opposite for days, watching, waiting for people to re-emerge, even looked for alternative entrances and exits, nothing." He paused. "I waited for the young man to leave and investigated."

"You broke in?" I heard the pitch change in my voice. "Bill that's dangerous!"

"I know, I know, but it was what I found that made me scarper." His voice changed.

"Bill, what did you find?" I asked, not sure if I wanted to know.

"Blood. Blood and possessions from the people that went in but never came out. He had cleaned well, but I know that metallic smell like the back of my hand." His voice quivered in fear. "As soon as I smelt that, I checked his chair. It's a barber chair Mags, and there was the scent of blood on it. I left as soon as I smelt that. And I knew I had to call you."

I sat in silence. Had we found it? The reason to go in. But that would put Bill in extreme danger, if anyone had seen him enter and told the young man who was now that so called barber...he could be next on that killer's list.

"Mags, you still there?" Bill sounded as though he was beginning to panic.

"Still here, digesting." I said softly. It didn't explain where the bodies were and wouldn't explain how they made it to Iris Rouse. "Bill, was there a chute under the chair?"

"I didn't stick around long enough to look Mags," He paused. "Barber of Fleet Street, this is all sounding way too familiar."

"I know." I said quietly. "Bill could you come in?" I asked, I was worried for Jeffries' wellbeing, he could be next.

"When?" Was all he asked. I guess he could tell by my voice.

"As soon as you physically can."

"Look up." I glanced up, smiling and hanging up the phone as I saw a tired, sickened, appalled and disturbed Bill Jeffries. The others were also smiling, the team members greeted Bill as though he was still a member of the team.

"Bill!" I shook his hand. "It is good to see you. Despite the circumstances."

"It is, I wish they were better." I motioned to the seat that he every so often took. "So, could there have been a chute under the chair, if I am thinking what you are, is someone recreating The Demon Barber of Fleet Street?"

He nodded; I took my time to really look at him. Retirement had done him some good, though not all.

"We believe that something will happen in two nights Bill." I told him simply. "A ritual of some kind."

"How did you get there?" I pointed outside, the lights flickered wildly again as if someone was throwing a fit of anger, the buzzing began angrier than before. "That has been happening since you went on your leave, that is the worst it's been. There are also links, join us in a little while. We are collating all the facts now. Before we decide and therefore take them down. We think it could be planned for Halloween."

I smiled at his dumbstruck. "Believe me Bill if I thought this was normal circumstances, I wouldn't have even considered a ritual, but it is not a coincidence."

He looked thoughtful and joined the team as we discussed all we had found. I did now and again glance over at Jeffries, he tensed at certain descriptions and blanched when we showed the woman and the young man in recent murders and throughout history. He also scoffed at the idea that the woman throughout history and the woman who we thought was the more recent one, were the same people. I knew he would. But he didn't utter a word until the end.

"Well, that all sounds well and good, but how are you going to stop them?" That was all he said. "Because, the minute you go to them on the defensive, someone is going to get hurt." I saw a glance towards me. I knew what he meant. I didn't want anyone on my team to get hurt because of this. I had already done this, and I still bore the scars, both physically and mentally. A psychologist would have a field day with my brain.

As we spoke the sun went down, day had turned to night. One day more.

But around seven pm, we had a plan, all of us. Including Barnett and Jeffries, just like old times. We had decided, that with a lot of prosthetics and fake blood, one of the men would become the latest 'victim' and would signal to us using a radio. They would also have their gun hidden, as a self defence mechanism, in case the killer came at them again. The rest of us would be stationed either at the meat pie place and at the café across the road. Hopefully, they would then show where the bodies went, and how they made it to the meat pie place if Rouse was indeed involved, then she as well as the accomplice doing the killing would be arrested and this whole thing could be put behind us. Or so we thought.

We hadn't thought that the two would be closed for business on Halloween. Clearly, I had been wrong. Both the barber and the meat pie place were closed. We sat for hours in the café until closing opposite the barbers, and at a small pub near the meat pie place. Then due to the places closing, we had to rethink our plan, and how we would go about it.

I offered with the support of Jeffries or Barnett, to go to one of the following, the bar or club and see whether they appeared there. Barnett was all for it. Jeffries had to get back home to his children, I had forgotten with him being there, that he wasn't a member of the team anymore. He assured me he would keep an eye on the next few days on the places and let us know if anything changed.

We thanked him as Barnett, and I went to the bar and then the club. Neither of the two were there, we stuck around until both closed. The reconvened at the station. We had come to a dead end, with an uncertainty to it. Had I been wrong? Was the ritual not a real thing? Had the couple just been there at the right time? Barnett and I had arrived back at the station at the same time, I had sparked up a cigarette, blowing the smoke into the air when he arrived.

We stood in silence. The only thing that was heard was our breathing. Inhale, Exhale, Inhale smoke, Exhale smoke.

When I had finished, stumped out the cigarette we went inside. What we found was our team in bits and out in the corridor. Our room had been trashed and this time it was more severe. Our computer screens had been smashed, thrown to the floor and the light hung from the rafters by a single wire.

The team luckily had managed to escape with barely a scratch. Some more traumatised than others. But they all stood together proudly when they saw us. They explained that they had come back to write the reports of the day when everything went dark, they were assaulted by something as it crashed through the room. They had left quickly, not wanting to be killed by the glass shards that had flown everywhere and the light that threatened them from above. Whatever or whoever had done this was angry. Livid with our poking around and prodding. They had been enraged by what we had uncovered and now their wrath was shown.

As I walked through the broken room, I wondered. Had this been a supernatural being, or had the couple come here while we had been out and started to destroy what we had found, before the team had returned, thus extinguishing the lights and hurting those within the room before the team left. Were they still in there biding their time until we left, and they could risk coming out of hiding? When I asked the front desk for brooms, dustpans and brushes, and asked for someone to remove the hanging light, I questioned whether someone or some people had entered the room before the others, I was told as a broom cupboard was pointed out, and an electrician on the way that no-one apart from the team had entered that room.

I showed nothing on my face as I swept the glass shards, tinkling into my dustpan. The team should think that someone was in the room, it seemed more believable than a supernatural force coming in and destroying everything and hurting them. In that moment I believed. I believed that something evil was in Whitechapel, and it was now stalking us, me, my team.

Now I was not a religious woman by any account but that night I visited my local church, sat on those hard, unmovable pews and I prayed. Prayed to anyone who would hear my pleas. Pleas to keep my team, my colleagues, my now friends safe. With everything I had. I stayed there for hours. In silence, hands clenched tight. I wanted my team, my friends and colleagues to be safe. No matter the cost to my own life. I was an Abberline, this is what we did. We made sure our loved ones were safe, no matter the cost to us. It was what my ancestor had done, he had played the system's game and lost a lot. His respect for his name, his second wife and child, his home eventually. I would be the same. I was an Abberline. I would do anything for my loved ones. Anything.

Chapter 21

No answer came. I wasn't surprised, no-one answered the Abberline line.

I went home, begrudgingly, and when I saw what awaited me there, I turned around and left, I didn't enter my building. Not that there was much there. I had a wallet, my coat and my keys. That was all, left from the broken husk that was my building. I hoped that my neighbours had been just as lucky, and none had been in the building when it had caught a flame. I had nowhere to go but back to the station, in the pitch black, where I lit a candle, sitting there watching the flame. It danced and dived. A mystifying dance, that made me realise that there wasn't much left of my life at this point. Luckily, I had no other forms of possessions, I had not many clothes in the first place, my uniform stayed in my locker at the station, and the little plainsclothes I had were easily replaceable. The only thing I mourned was my grandfather clock. Nothing remained of it. That I was sure of. I would go back in the morning when the light was kinder, and I could see the damage in full.

"Mags?" I looked up; a shadow stood in the doorway. They came into the light, it was Jack.

"Jack? What are you doing here?" I asked. His face looked shocked.

"Could ask you the same?" He said sitting heavily.

"My flat had been torched." I replied. "I had nowhere else to go." I sighed, he looked terrified. "What about you?" I asked again.

"I came back to make sure it was all locked up. Then I saw you." He reached over to touch my hand. "I'm sorry about your flat, don't you have anywhere you can stay?"

I shook my head, thankful at least I wasn't alone. I sighed, leaning back in my chair.

"Did you have most things on you?" He asked.

"My wallet, keys and coat." I replied. I rubbed my forehead; I was bone tired. My chair felt like the only source of where I would be sleeping until Jack said.

"You can come and sleep on my couch for the night. My parents are out of town, they're visiting family up north, a good thing really." He sighed. "God that felt weird saying that."

I reached across and squeezed his hand in gratitude. "Thank you, Jack, that is kind and don't think of it. You're a member of my team, asking your D.I who has just lost her home is being a kind friend and colleague. Nothing more."

He smiled in relief and squeezed my hand back. Then he stood, I followed blowing out the candle on my way out, we locked up and Jack walked me back to his. He opened the door, let me in and proceeded to grab me blankets from the airing cupboard, a pillow from his parents' room and helped me get set up on the coach.

"I think mum had some spare clothes that you can use for sleeping, that way we can wash what your wearing tonight and then they will be fresh as a daisy in the morning." Jack said. "I'll run and get them, the bathroom is on the first floor in case you wanted to shower or have a bath, just leave your clothes outside and I shall put them in the wash, I'll leave a clean towel in the bathroom before I go and get my mum's stuff and I shall leave it outside. Have you eaten? Or would you like a cup of tea?"

I put a hand up to stop him. He was beginning to ramble, and he paused. "Thank you, Jack, a bath sounds heavenly, and I am a little hungry but don't put yourself out, it is late."

"I wouldn't be sleeping yet, I never can, and never Mags, I want to help as much as I can, so go have a bath, I'll run up and grab a towel and leave in there for you, then you can soak, I'll get clothes in and the kettle on. What would you like to eat?" Jack smiled, he seemed genuinely happy to help me and I would let him.

"A sandwich is fine Jack." I smiled. "Again, thank you."

"Anytime Mags, anytime."

As I soaked, I realised that Jack was a kind soul, he may have been several years my junior but there was something about him that made him an old soul. I could hear the washing machine spinning meaning he had got my clothes in quick and they were finishing the cycle now before he put them in the dryer, I heard him singing in the kitchen as well. That made me chuckle, he always was able to make everyone laugh. That was one of the best things about him.

After my soak, I towelled dry and placed the borrowed clothes on before taking the towel down and meeting Jack in the kitchen. He was busy over the stove. Cooking something, an empty Tupperware box sat on the side.

"That smells nice." I said, making him jump slightly. "Sorry Jack, I didn't mean to make you jump."

"That's ok Mags," He said, spotting the towel, he added "You didn't need to bring that down, I could have done that in the morning."

"I was raised to do such things." I smiled.

"Your sandwich Madam." He grabbed the sandwich from the fridge and placed on the side, with a flourish. I chuckled as I sat at the breakfast bar while he worked, eating the sandwich and sipping the tea he had made. He grabbed the towel and threw it next to the washing machine.

"Thanks again Jack," I said, once I had finished, it was surprising how hungry I had been.

"No problem." He whisked the plate away and began washing up before I could protest.

"Jeez Jack, you could have at least let me wash up." I joked.

"Nope, you're the guest," He smiled. It was surprising how much he followed those views. "Besides, Mum always said that I would make a mean bed and breakfast owner." He laughed.

I laughed, I could see it, if he hadn't been a police officer, I could see him with a bed and breakfast. I wanted to know more, but was unsure, would it seem out of place to ask him about himself outside of work? I was his senior after all, it wasn't appropriate.

He saw the look on my face and answered for me, turning away, checking what he was cooking. "I can cook, mum taught me since I was young, I use it much you use smoking as an outlet. It helps me think, it helps me to work things out." His back was to me, but I knew that he was no longer smiling. "With everything that has happened, from when you were nearly killed, to the multiple murders we have dealt with together, I found cooking meals and placing them in the fridge has helped." He sighed. "It's been an eye opener, that's for sure. And it's also made me wonder about you Mags." He turned back to me. I could see the worry in his face. "You do so much for us as a team, but there is no one looking out for you, and I vowed when I became Sergeant to do just that." He blushed. "Jeffries did it on the sly, but I know you don't appreciate that. But if you need anything Mags, you only must ask," He paused, a cheeky smile glittering his eyes. "Even if it is to stay at Chez Jack."

I laughed. Jack sure knew how to change something serious to a joke. If I had ever wanted to marry, when I wasn't to my job, someone like Jack would have been perfect. I sighed, there was no such thing.

"Penny for your thoughts." He laughed.

I laughed, "Worth more than that."

"Why's that?" He asked, perching on the side.

"Because their thoughts about you." I saw him blush and laughed. "Don't worry Jack, not in that way. Just if I ever married, I would hope I would hope he was like you." His blush darkened. He mumbled something but I didn't catch it. He turned and silently began moving what he had cooked into the Tupperware pot.

He was unusually quiet, that worried me.

"Jack? Did I say something wrong?" I said concerned "I didn't mean it- "

"No, Mags, it's me. I'm being silly." He shook his head. Then glanced at the clock on the wall. "It's getting late though. You should think about sleeping."

I shook my head. "Not until you tell me what's going on." I crossed my arms.

He sighed. Blushed again and then said in a rush. "Ilikeyouok,morethanmyD.I."

I knew my raised eyebrow made him recheck himself. He sighed. His face was beetroot red. "Mags, I like you ok, I like you more than I should as my D.I." He turned away and I could only sit there in shock.

"But...I am far older than you Jack, and- "

"I know, but that doesn't bother me, age is merely a number. But I have always wanted to keep work and personal lives separate." The tips of his ears were now beetroot too, to match his face most likely.

"I don't know what to say." I said quietly. It was the first time in my very lonely life that I had even been thought of as desirable. Not even the first boyfriend I had ever had, had thought of me that way.

"You don't need to say anything." Jack said. "But you should go rest. I'm going to finish up here and then head up and shower." His hands were shaking though his voice was steady. And before I could stop him, he had finished with the Tupperware, popped it inside the fridge and had disappeared up the stairs. I sat there in shock. I didn't know what to say, didn't know what to do. I was flattered that was sure, but he was the sergeant on my team, a much younger person. Who knew?!

I couldn't sleep that night, I lay awake, thinking over Jack's words. How long had this gone on for? He never showed more than that while we worked, this was all a true shock. But then I could see his point of view, from where he was, it was probably because I was one of the only women on the team that he could see as whatever material, and Lucy had not longed joined, but maybe that wasn't his point of view at all. I groaned. I needed a cigarette. I rose from the sofa and fished in my coat pocket, luckily, I still had a packet of cigarettes and a lighter. I opened the back garden and lit a cigarette, the orange light sparking up the porch.

"Couldn't sleep?" Came a voice beside me. In his hand Jack also had a cigarette. I had jumped a mile.

"No." I panted. "You scared me though."

"Sorry."

We stood there in silence, smoking. The navy sky was still a dark, a few stars winked at us, and I knew I would have a hard job getting back to sleep. So, I knew I would be awake now for the rest of the night until the sky lightened.

Our smoke mingled in the air.

"I didn't know you smoked?" I said finally, hating the silence.

"Oh, it's an on, off thing. Felt like I needed one tonight." He said quietly. "Mags, what I said, just forget about it." He flicked the ash off the cigarette. "Let's just be workers, I have liked you for a very long time, and I could have chosen a better time, but with everything going on...I needed to tell you. But just forget it." He blushed again.

"Jack, how can I forget it?" I said, just as quietly.

"I'll transfer out if it makes you uncomfortable." His voice was resigned.

"No!" I almost shouted in the still air. He looked stunned. "You're a damn good sergeant, it would be saddening to see you go." He sighed. I think he was expecting more, so I took the goddamn chance. It would play on my mind later, but what the hell!

I put out my cigarette and kissed him full on the lips.

He didn't respond for a while and then I felt him, put down the cigarette, stump it out and then his arms went around my waist, pulling me tighter to him, my hands on his shoulders. It was strange at first, but then it connected something. Something warm, something I hadn't experience in a long time. I felt his hands trace my back, light and sensual. When we broke for breath, he smiled. That smile. It was warm, it was filled with longing. He was about to pull away when I pulled him to me again, more forcefully. He seemed dazed, but that soon faded when he kissed me back just as passionately.

"Mags, are you sure about this?" He panted when we had broken apart for the second time. I showed him just how ok I was with it. I traced his face, and down his chest, gripping his t-shirt tight. He chuckled. I felt that in his chest, it was a pleasant feeling. "Ok, but let's go inside. It's cold out here."

"Is it? I hadn't noticed." I laughed. He placed an arm around me, ushering me inside, locking the back door. Still thinking of safety. Even at a time like this.

"Mags?" He was looking at me, and I took a good long look at him, he had aged since the Ripper murders, a small beard and he had muscled out since I had first arrived. His voice was filled with worry, as if I was going to change my mind. I smiled at him. He smiled. "Good night Mags." He said with finality. "I will see you in the morning." He went to leave but I grabbed his hand, pulling him back to me.

"Oh no you don't." I joked. "You started something; you finish it."

He chuckled. "Is that so?" It was soft.

"Yes." His hand, the one that was free traced my face, and then stroked my neck,and down to my shoulders.

"But I was trying to be a gentleman." I laughed softly. "And wait to officially date you."

"Is that so?" I parroted. His hands caressed down to my hips. I shivered, not with cold but with a feeling. He was smiling the whole time. The hand in mine, left it and went to the other hip, pulling me to him. I gripped his t-shirt again.

He kissed me; it was like he had a fire within him that needed extinguishing with my lips. His hands roved up and down, to my neck, caressing my skin, until the rested back onto my hips, his grip on them tightening. My grip on his t-shirt was just as tight, my other hand, was around his neck. Then his kisses went from my lips to my neck, the crook, where it was sensitive. I moaned softly, and I felt him smile. He continued kissing each side of my neck. I felt a warmth begin to pool in my stomach. I hadn't been kissed like this in a long time, made to feel desirable. I raised the hand on his neck to his hair, ruffling it and the other hand caressed his chest through his t-shirt, he shivered. His hands, lightly moved over my breasts and I moaned, arching my back. He chuckled, his fingers now caressing the buds under my shirt. My legs began to feel like jelly. Before long, he had pulled me into his arms, bridal style and took me upstairs to his bedroom. There he laid me on the bed and continued to do what he had been doing, I moaned again. Again, he chuckled, I realised I wanted his t-shirt off. So, my hands went to take his t-shirt off, he paused briefly to allow me to remove it from his head before resuming, this time with his mouth through the shirt. The warmth began to build again. I moaned louder, his hands caressing the sides of my breasts through the material. My fingers roved over his own buds and I felt him jerk at the touch, but soon he too began moaning into my chest.

I took that opportunity to then move and pin him underneath me. Time for payback, he was smiling brightly, his eyes filled with lust. I moved my mouth to his buds and did to him what he did to me, kissing and caressing his chest. He removed my borrowed over my head, and I was then in a bra, trousers before him, before he pinned me again, kissing me deeply. I could feel him through the thin trousers I wore, and the shorts he wore. And I smiled, into his lips my hands went to touch him, but he grabbed them and held them together over my head.

"Nope." He chuckled.

And then he unhooked my bra, kissing down to my navel. I was surprised. Pleasantly so. Who would have thought I would be here right now? I certainly hadn't and I wasn't sorry either.

Like lightning the trousers were also pulled off me and I lay naked, suddenly I felt self-conscious and tried to cover myself up, he shook his head. And kissed me deeply again. Showing me rather than telling me there was no need to hide, he thought I was beautiful. When I moaned into his mouth, he left me, kissing down to my inner thighs, and then he was suddenly...there. I gasped in delight as his crafty mouth undid me. I felt my hands fist his bedcovers. I felt him chuckle...still right there. And it sent vibrations through me. Undoing me again, and when his fingers replaced him, my back arched, so high that it nearly arched off the bed. He was over me again, his fingers still there. Dancing inside of me, lightly touching the bud of pleasure I knew was down there. And when that undid me for several times, he kissed me, withdrawing them. I whimpered. Wetness was all I felt down there. He moved from me for a manner of seconds, removed his shorts and placed himself at my entrance. He paused. "Are you sure Mags?" He said huskily. "We can stop."

"No." I said, guiding him in, he jerked at my touch. He filled me to the brim, I arched up to meet him, pushing him in deeper. He groaned, I moaned with him. Then he started to move, slowly at first but gaining momentum as we had a rhythm established. I raked my short nails over his back, my legs wrapping around his waist, pushing him further with a deep growl.

"Mags." He growled. "Oh, beautiful Mags, you have no idea." He panted, "How long."

"Long enough clearly." I panted in return, his lips going to my breast again, causing me to come undone. He soon followed. We lay there, he on top of me, sweat glistening off him, panting, gasping for our breathing to regain itself. He was not finished, not by how he still felt inside.

"Mags."He said, his voice hoarse. "I-"I cut him off with a kiss. I heard him groan into my mouth, using that as a surprise, I flipped him over, so that this time I rode him. He seemed stunned. That was until I moved, he groaned, his head thrown back. I watched him. He looked in thrall. I wiggled my hips a little, a gasp pulled from his throat and I giggled. His hands went to my hips, thumbs then brushed my inner thighs. I threw back my own head, the rhythm grew again. Then his hands moved again, to cup my breasts, thumbs brushing those now puckered buds. I moaned deeply. He groaned, hips bucking inside me. And then he flipped me, pushing inside me hard, I screamed his name at that. That undid him, he moved faster, moaning my name. And then we undid together. This time we lay there, panting, gasping, hoarse. I could feel him deflate.

I knew I had no worries with the off chance of an accidental pregnancy, a depo injection, a mere month ago had stopped that, when I finally allowed my brain to catch up with what happened. He raised himself slowly onto his arms, looking down at me. I saw him connect the dots too, but I shook my head, "Injection." I said softly. He sighed in relief. But then he looked at me again and smiled lazily. "That was." He breathed.

"Yes." No more words were needed. I closed my eyes, feeling him lay his head on my chest, my breathing deep and harsh. I knew my heart was beating wildly, a drum inside the chest. I knew he also could hear it. But I bet that his was doing the exact same thing.

"Do you regret it?" Came his small voice. He wasn't looking at me, that much I knew, he was talking to my heart. I opened my eyes. How could I regret an act such as that?

"No Jack." I replied, raising his head to look at me. His eyes looked so sad. "I don't regret that, do you?"

He just shook his head. I smiled. "Then there is no need to worry." He moved off me, and pulled me to his side, arm going around me. I lay there, a hand on his chest, feeling his chest rise and fall. He was thinking, I knew it, but in the moments when I thought I would regret it, I thought about what this meant for work. Departmental relationships weren't frowned upon but would a D.I and the Sergeant? It would be something to investigate. Then I would step down if the case came that we were not allowed to be together. For once I was not choosing my job. I would do something like Jeffries did if push came to shove. And that was an unusual thought. Had I found something worth more than my job for once?

His hand traced shapes on my hips, forcing my gaze to his. "Penny for your thoughts." He asked, a smug smile on his face.

"Again, their worth more than a penny, as they are about you." I replied smiling.

He chuckled. "Really?"

"Yes, thinking about whether it would be ok for us to have this with work." His hand paused.

"Huh?"

"I want this Jack." I said. I felt him shift, to that he was sitting. My stomach lurched. Did he only want what had just happened? Was that it now?

I gulped silently and slowly moved off the bed. I began picking up my borrowed clothes. I could feel the sting of tears, had I been stupid again?

"Mags, what are you doing?" He sounded confused.

"Grabbing my stuff, borrowed that it may be, so I can clean up and head down to the couch." I said, fighting back the tears.

"Why?" He asked, pulling me up to face him. My reflection showed in his puzzled eyes. "You can stay up here. You don't need clothes though." He tried to joke. But he saw my expression. "What's wrong?"

"Was it just about the sex?" I asked quietly. "You soon moved when I said I wanted this. Do you not?"

He seemed puzzled then realisation dawned on him. "Mags, I'm sorry I was just shocked, I thought it was only me, but you shocked me. I guess I reacted badly, I'm sorry." He pulled me to him again. Titled my head up to his and kissed me. When we stopped, he said stroking my cheek. "I definitely want this." Soft. His voice was soft. "Stay, we can work the particulars out when we get to that." He continued. "Because I want *you*." He pulled the clothes from my hands, dropping them on the floor, pulling me back to the bed, laying me down, turning off the lights, but leaving a single candle lit, and drew me to him.

Chapter 22

After a night full of joy and surprises. I awoke the next morning to more. I awoke alone, though I heard the shower running. I smiled, we had eventually fallen asleep, but before that well...I understood the stamina of the youth. I chuckled to myself. I wondered whether I should join him in the shower but trying to move well...that wasn't happening anytime soon. I ached. I lay there, inching myself slowly off the bed, when he came back into the room in just a towel. He smiled, seeing me awake.

"Did I wake you?" He asked as he towel dried his hair.

"No." I said, "My body did, but I can't move." The cocky smile that met my words, well he could be cocky. "Just give me a hand."

"Thought I did." He smiled like the cat that got the cream. I threw a pillow at him, and he laughed. "Alright, I'll help you." And he did, picking me up bridal style with ease and taking me to the bathroom, he left while I used the toilet and I managed to grab a shower, that eased the aches and pains. At some point he had popped his head in and left me a towel. He had also left the dry clothes on the side for me so I could change as soon as I had dried off.

On my journey down to the kitchen, a coffee steaming and a dancing Jack at the kitchen stove.

"Nice moves." I said sitting at the breakfast bar. He turned and smiled.

"That's what you said last night." He really was a cat that had got the cream.

"Sssh, coffee." I said, smiling into the rich beans in front of me, then a plate slid in front of me. Bacon, eggs, mushrooms and toast. "Jack?"

"Thought you might like a fry up." He blushed. I stood and went around and kissed him.

"Thank you." I returned and dug in with gusto.

I was ready for that, not just because of the night I had, but because I was always hungry in the morning. A girl could get used to this, but I was determined not to let it interfere in work. We had discussed it last night, until our research had been complete, the case done, we would only see each other when we could. That way no-one could accuse us of the relationship, I would study whether a D.I and a Sergeant could date on the same team and he would not pretend but act as though he wasn't imagining us together in the Biblical sense. I would struggle to do the same. I was happy, happier than I had ever been in my life, even though my grandfather clock was burned, and I had nowhere to live. Jack had agreed while I was out of house and his parents were away, that I could stay with him, though to the others I would be on his couch. It would have been too much to afford a hotel or B N B every night until I found a place. One that I could easily afford that is. I would have been pushed as it was. I could never ask my family for help, considering the fiasco that, that would cause.

I then took a cigarette and my lighter from my coat pocket, Jack had finished his breakfast and was washing up, he nodded that he would be out when he had dried his hands, I had sparked up when he came out. He borrowed my lighter and lit his own. We stood in companionable silence, until his arm snaked around my waist. I leaned in. Grateful for him being there, and knew I would miss this at work, I was sure he would make up for it though when we could be seen together. He would take me on dates, he had already told me that. I didn't think our ages were an issue and whoever said they were, well they had no need to stick their noses in our business.

Jack insisted on the way to the station that we swing by my flat and see the true damage and see if there was anything to salvage. There were a bunch of fire engines still there, and some members of the police force. When they spotted me, they came over a look of shock on their face.

"Sorry Ma'am, we heard your flat was one of the ones that was burnt, there is nothing remaining. The fire department are trying to find the cause, but right now the suspected thing is someone lit a flame inside as a lot of gas leaked, we suspected it was the people above you." I could feel Jack behind me, in his Sergeant role, the role we would play until we could. I felt him place a hand on my shoulder and I wanted nothing more than to turn and cry into his chest, but I bit back the tears and faced the officer with dignity.

"Was anything salvaged? Like a grandfather clock?" I had to ask. But the officers faced showed the truth.

"I'm afraid not Ma'am, the insurance will cover all that you have lost, but we found nothing remaining, not even the grandfather clock."

"It's alright." I turned to Jack. "We best get to the station, there's nothing to do here."

He nodded, and we headed to work.

Before we went in, he handed me a cigarette. We paused outside, and I smoked, mourning the los of my home and my inheritance from my grandfather.

"It'll be ok Mags, you have somewhere to stay." I could hear him try to cheer me up.

"That grandfather clock, was my inheritance from my grandfather Jack, my family and I well, we don't get on and that was the only thing I received from them, when he passed. Now I don't have that." My hands shook slightly, but I tried to steel them. He grabbed my hand squeezing.

"You don't need to explain, but I am here, just like the team. Lucky really you weren't inside when it happened." He pondered.

I just nodded and finished my cigarette. He let go of my hand, nodded that he would be inside and went in. I lowered my stiff shoulders from being up and proud to saddened. What I had, was gone. I was lucky, that I wasn't in there when it happened and that I had a great team and someone who cared. I took a final drag on my cigarette, stumped it out on the ground, remembering what I was thankful for, raised my head and shoulders again and walked in with my head held high, the only sign of my pain was my eyes.

On entering the room, smiles met me. I smiled in return.

"Mags, are we trying the plan again?" I heard Barnett ask.

I nodded. "Yes, we shall keep trying. We may have failed but we need to try again. We shall do it in stages. Two go to the meat pie place, two to the barbers. Two shall wait here."

"I'll go to the meat pie place." Barnett and Max said in unison, I nodded.

"I'll go to the barbers." Oliver and Lucy said.

"I'll go and sit periodically in the cafes opposite." Amy said.

"I'll stay here." Jack said. I nodded to all of them.

"Clock in every ten minutes with myself and Jack, keep us updated, we will swap out in thirty minutes once you have got there." They nodded and went straight out in their teams.

I went to my office and pulled up the files I had first received when entering this station, about relationships within a team and department, while Jack was re-reading notes. It kept me busy and he knew that what I needed right now was to be kept as busy as possible. But every so often he would bring me a coffee as I did my research.

Ten minutes later, the first team clocked in. "We're here." Then the second team clocked in. "We're here." Then Amy. "Here Ma'am."

In position we waited, I printed out the piece I needed, placing it in my pocket, before Jack and I left the station. Ready to relieve someone on the other teams. We separated, though I could tell that pained him. But he knew whoever was on my team would keep me safe.

I went to the barbers. He went to the meat pie. I knew that Oliver and Lucy would report anything they had seen. Amy was currently at the café opposite there. A coffee sat in front of her, to maintain appearances, I sat opposite and got one myself. "How has it been?" I asked. We looked like to friends catching up.

"Quiet." Amy said, "Oliver and Lucy have been wandering the church next door, keeping an eye on the door, they have been texting me."

"Good. Nothing to report then."

"Not yet, but we are keeping optimistic." Amy smiled, her coffee finished she rose and said that she would swap with Lucy, Oliver would make his way to the meat pie place and Max would join Amy. I would stay where I was and hoped that the others would work out a good routine. I sat and read the piece I had printed before I had left, it was helpful and outlined the relationships one could have while on a team. It was allowed for a D.I and a sergeant in the same department to date, there were rules however, it was not to cloud their professional judgement, neither of them could put their personal feelings above their job, they could not favour the person they were dating above everyone else in the team. Jack and I had no qualms about being separated from work, we knew it was our jobs.

"Checking in." Barnett called. "You ok Mags?"

"Yeah, sitting and reading." I replied, "One eye on the place." It was the truth in between reading I would stop, sip my cooling coffee and watch the barbers. Every so often I saw Max or Amy appear around the church.

"Good. I will go to the station; shall I ask Amy to come with me?" He questioned.

"Yes, Max can swap with me and I will head there." I finished my coffee, grabbed the paper, paid the bill and stuffed the paper in my pocket before leaving. But as I did so there was movement in the barbers. Max had messaged me, saying someone was coming out. I paused, pretending I was window shopping and watched the mans reflection go past me in the window. He was heading towards the meat pie place. His face looked thunderous. When he had passed, I called the team.

"He's left, headed towards the meat pie place." I hung up and slowly walked behind him, keeping him in my sight. I briefly saw Max, Amy and Barnett on the opposite side, walking together. Amy and Max were arm in arm, pretending they were a couple, Barnett strode behind them, window shopping like I was. Then I realised, someone needed to go back to the barbers. So I turned around, texting Barnett to come with me.

We made our way back to the barbers, realising he had left the door unlocked in his rampage to leave. Cautiously we entered. The chair in the middle of the room, caught my attention. I hovered around it. And then Barnett gave a squeak, he pointed to the marks around the chair, it was like a trapdoor. We had found where the bodies went after they left the chair, did we risk going down there? Deciding against, we left, making sure no one saw us enter or leave, leaving the door exactly as it had been when the suspect had left, then we walked arm in arm to the meat pie place, unhooking when we met up with the team.

"The chair has a trapdoor underneath." Barnett said. "We went in, he had left the door unlocked."

I nodded. I didn't trust myself to speak, but Oliver did it for me.

"So, we found where the bodies go but not how they get to the pie place. He wasn't carrying anything, so it must be…underground?" He paused.

Barnett almost crowed. "The tunnels!" He said in an excited whisper. "Where the previous barber of Fleet Street took his victims, he must have someone else, who is down there, cleaning and running the body parts to the pie place."

Amy then said. "But who?"

We thought. Then I spoke. "Whoever it is, if we find them, then we can prove everything, but it would be someone being threatened or coerced. So, we have to take that into account."

They nodded.

"Let's go back to the station." I said to Barnett, we can look those tunnels up. Then when we need to, we can swap with someone else who can continue them."

"Mags, could I not go?" Amy asked. "I want to help." I nodded, smiling at her.

"Ok Amy, go with Barnett, see what you can find." I turned to the two who had been at the pie shop for most of the morning, "You two head to the barbers. I'll stay here."

Pained smiles met me, mainly from Jack but they followed the orders, before he left, I touched Jack's arm. "Talk later." I added. "Found it."

He nodded smiling and left. I hoped he would stay safe.

Oliver remained with me and we went around the back, while Lucy sat at the front. We looked for any sign of a secret entrance or delivery slot big enough for body parts or parts of flesh. When we found none, we walked round the front, raving about the meat pies we were going to eat. Even if the thought of them made me feel physically sick.

When evening came and we had all made our rounds to both places we reconvened back at the station, it seemed like an exhausting day even if we hadn't apprehended anyone. But we were so much closer. There was a third person, we knew that, but finding them was going to be the tough thing. If we found them then this case would be wrapped up. We would have our evidence and the suspects would be locked up.

I saw an exhausted yet persevering team in front of me. I thanked them for their hard work today and told them to rest up, another long day met us tomorrow, Jack followed me into my office, where I asked him to close the door.

"Mags?" He asked, a nervous smile on his face.

"Sit Jack." I smiled in return, I hoped it was a reassuring one. "I found something."

He sat, but I could see he was nervous.

"We are allowed." Was all I said, his face lighting up, nerves vanishing. "But it mustn't cloud our professional judgements, we should not show favouritism."

"No chance of that." He chuckled. "But that is good news." He sighed. "I want nothing more than to kiss you right now."

I chuckled. "And I you, but let's wait till we get home yeah?"

Home. Something I hadn't felt in a long time. Then I realised. "When do your parents get home?"

"I'm not sure." He fidgeted. "They left and said they would return soon, but if I know my parents, they are too busy enjoying themselves to think about coming back."

"You need to call them." I said softly. "I am pretty sure they don't want to return and see a stranger in their home."

"I'll call them now. Let me know when your ready to leave and we will head." He said standing and leaving the office. Before he opened the door, he blew me a kiss. Then left to call his parents.

I sighed. I was happy, but still we were in the honeymoon stage of our relationship. Sooner or later the team would need to be made aware, and their reactions I wasn't sure on. I didn't want to lose their respect, so the news could wait until we had caught these suspects.

A few days later, we had done just that. It was a lot of waiting around between that, but our plan came through for us. Barnett had offered this time to be the body, carrying a small gun that we had loaned him, only for self defence purposes, that I had, had to ask permission for from the chief. He had agreed, if only to get me out of his office. The paperwork was soon filled in, and Barnett had hidden the gun on his leg. Hidden beneath his trousers. When he had gone in, we moved, surrounding the barber shop, and waited until we heard a slam. Then we moved, we caught the barber covered in blood, the fake blood and arrested him. Him in handcuffs, sulking led us to the underground chamber where the stench of rotting corpses met us. Barnett was there too, horror-struck but alive, to the barber's surprise, and the barber showed us somewhat unwillingly where the runner hid, he seemed relieved to be free, and showed Jack and Oliver where the two connecting places met. He would run the sliced-up body parts that the barber had done, and where they would then go to the meat pie place. Oliver, Amy and Lucy took the suspect we had to the station, where he would sit in a cell, myself, Jack and a blood-stained Barnett made our way to the meat pie place. Barnett and I below, Jack above, when she appeared panicked into the area that had been cordoned off as her receiving end, I lunged, arresting her on abetting and aiding a murderer, food hygiene and using body parts in her food.

Her meat pie shop was closed down, the barber shop searched, and we found artefacts that had been people's possessions, which we handed to the parents and families, along with the bodies that had been cleaned and placed in closed caskets for them.

We had been hailed as heroes. As successes.

Our suspects would rot in jail and we would carry on.

Or so we thought…

Chapter 23

Jack and I had told the team, who were ecstatically happy for us. We made them aware that because of this, there would be no favouritism, and we would be professional at work.

I also had called Jeffries, who though surprised congratulated us.

The runner from the shop had been detained in jail, for aiding and abetting under duress, but he would be allowed to leave after his probation sentence had been finished.

Jack and I were on our first date when our phones rang.

"Rain check." We both said, laughing as we asked for the bill in the restaurant, we were in.

"D.I Abberline."

"Ma'am, they've escaped."

"How?" I said sharply, making Jack wince. "How could this have happened?"

"The night guard then checked on them, something hit him, and he was blacked out. They escaped."

"How, that place is locked up tight."

"We know, the hunt is still on for them, but we wanted to let you and your team know." They hung up.

I sighed; we never got a break.

"What's up Mags?" Jack asked.

"They've escaped."

"How the heck!" He said, and then sighed, standing to his feet, helping me stand as well.

"My thoughts exactly."

"At the same time from separate places?" He asked, as we left the restaurant.

"Yes."

He swore, something I had never heard him do, not even when we were tracking the Ripper and before that.

"I'm sorry." He apologised. "I never swear but…"

"It's alright." I took his hand. "A few curse words are appropriate in this situation."

He tucked me under his arm as we made our way to the station, I changed at my locker into appropriate clothes and shoes. Jack had done the same, and together in a professional manner we walked down to where the prisoners had been held. The guard that had been attacked, sat an ice pack to his head and answering questions. When he saw us, he sighed heavily, us meant more questions.

"Don't worry, we just want to ask how this happened." Jack said crouching down in front of him.

"I don't know. All I knew is they were there when I did my rounds, next thing I know I'm hit with something to the back of the head and out cold, when I woke up, they were gone." He said hoarsely.

"Was there anyone here before that? A visitor?" I asked, crouching down beside Jack. The man thought for a moment and then winced. "It's alright if you can't remember. Don't force it." I added seeing the man's pain. I stood. I issued orders to the officers standing by, "Get a look on CCTV, see if anyone exited or entered the building before the escape, and see where they headed."

"Yes Ma'am." They saluted and got straight to it.

Jack chuckled. I gave him a questionable look. "Every time." He added. I shook at his obvious inflection towards an innuendo, as we made our way to give the regretful news to our team.

They were all stunned. Some- Amy and Lucy, went to look more closely at the site and the CCTV cameras, knowing that most of the police officers wouldn't know what they looked like in depth like they would. Barnett was the most dazed out of all of them. He even muttered something under his breath, extremely out of character. I found that suspicious. Barnett out of character, that was something I never thought I would see of him. I made a mental note to see whether he had visited the couple before they escaped. It would explain why he was acting like this. Had he helped them escape? Was he working for them the entire time? I shook my head forcefully, that was ludicrous! Barnett had been helping us, not hindering us, like someone with them would have been. But I had to ask.

"Joe? Did you go down there at all today?" I asked.

"No, although I will admit I wanted to, to ask them questions. But I didn't." I could see hurt flash across his eyes.

"That's fine. I am sure all of us would want to ask them similar questions." His answer was what I expected but he seemed fidgety, nervous for some unknown reason. That was also suspicious. I sighed, rubbing my temple.

"Until we find them, there's not much we can do at this point." I said, feeling a headache come on. "Some of us would be best going home."

"I'll stay." Jack and Max said. "We can send the girls home, they worked late last night."

I nodded. "I'll stay as well; in case something comes to light." I added.

"I'll head home too; shall I take Oliver with me?" Barnett asked.

"Please Joe, make sure that he knows that we shall swap tomorrow." I smiled. He smiled in return. A normal smile.

"See you tomorrow Mags." He waved.

"I'll go tell the girls they can head." Jack said softly. "Then I'll get a copy of the CCTV sent up so we can look from up here."

"Thanks Sergeant." I added.

"Anything for you Ma'am." The only change to our professional relationship, we made it very clear, that we were on the job. So, we used official titles. The tone, however, was aimed at me on a personal one.

Soon, as Jack was very good at his job as Sergeant, the CCTV tapes were sent up and each of us combed through one each. I made notes, officers, potential people of interest and then I saw something that made my stomach churn. One of them-Rouse, had merely stood up, looked up at the camera, waved and smiled with a smile with evil intent, then vanished. I asked Jack and Max to come in and watch the part I had. I watched their faces go from puzzled to terrified in a second.

"H-How?" Max stammered.

"Check the time. See if it happened to Eluf? If it has, then not only are we dealing with something sinister, but something that is unnatural." I said. They snapped to it, Jack's hand squeezing my shoulder ever so slightly.

A little while later, Max threw up.

"Max, you ok?" I asked coming out of the office. He merely pointed at the screen, I rewound it and I almost lost my dinner.

Rouse had appeared next to Eluf's cell. Then he too turned and grinned sinisterly at the camera, gave a royal wave, took Rouse's hand the pair disappeared. In the corner, was the guard, knocked out, how she had done that was not clear on the tape. Until Jack called us over.

"Ma'am, Max? You need to see this." His voice shook, fear and disgust.

"What-"But then on the screen made me freeze. We watched the guard turn around, smile Rouse's sinisterly evil smile and then collapsed. How? So maybe to him it had felt like being hit around the head. Had he been possessed? Was that a thing?

I knew the blood had drained from my face. I felt dizzy and light-headed, for the first time in my life I thought I would faint.

"Mags?" I heard Max say with a concerned tone, but he seemed far away.

"Ma'am? Ma'am? Mags?" Jack continued, then I felt him squeeze my hand, and I came back with a jolt.

"I'm alright." I said, though they could tell by my tone that I wasn't. "Best clear that up Max." I pointed to where he had lost his dinner, and I stood and shakily made my way to my office.

"Mags?" Jack asked again following me in, "You sure you're ok?"

"Not really." I sighed. "It's a shock, that's all."

"I'll say. Supernatural forces aren't usually in this job description." He sighed, sitting down.

"Your telling me." I sighed. "But how did they get out of there without anyone seeing that on the camera? Surely someone would have seen that unless.."My thought trailed. But Jack finished it.

"Unless that person watching was the one who has been working with them this whole time?!"

"We have to find that person!" Jack and I stood, racing downstairs. The night guard who had been attacked was still sitting, an ice pack to his head. We bypassed him and went into the security office. Two men were there.

"Hold it!" I shouted, "Who was in here when our two suspects escaped?" The two glanced at each other.

"Harry, no Josh, I am sure it was-" One joked.

"Cut it, who was it really?" I ordered. "Or I will suspend you on obstruction of justice!"

They gulped.

"Josh."

"Where is Josh now?" Jack asked.

"Beats me he clocked out an hour ago." The two men shrugged.

Jack and I glanced at each other, then we raced out of the room. We had to find Josh, he was the one who had been feeding the two-whatever they were our movements, and where we lived it seemed. All of us were in danger. Real danger.

In a small panic, I rang Barnett.

"Joe? Are you still with Oliver?" I breathed, panting.

"No, why?" He asked. "Mags, what's wrong?"

"We had a mole, in the station, the one watching the tape." I panted. "Ring Oliver, we are in serious danger."

"I'll get right on it; I'll ring Lucy and Amy too." He hung up.

Max was in the room, frozen by something. "Max?"

"I just got a call, and I recognised the address." He said numbly. "It's Amy. She's been attacked, her parents have been killed."

My hands went to my mouth. "Is Amy ok?" I asked.

"Shaken but managed to escape." Max said, "I'm going to go and meet her, bring her here."

"Good idea. See if you can get Lucy too."

I turned to Jack. "Your parents." I said. He nodded. His parents had returned the previous day, I had opted to stay elsewhere but they would have none of it. As they saw it they were happy their son had someone in his life, like me even if we were colleagues as well. And made sure that I was made to feel welcome. They were now in danger.

Jack rushed to call them. When he came back, awash with relief I smiled.

"They're safe, I told them to get out of the house and stay out." He said. "They are staying at a hotel, and I told them not to contact anyone, in case."

"Good call." I knew my parents were safe. We hadn't spoken in years so there was no way they would be a target. But Jack's parents were sweet, and I wished no harm on them. I prayed for the third time in my life. I prayed to God for help. To send someone to help us. I knew no one would probably come and that we were on our own, but I had to try.

Max came through not that long later and informed us he had managed to get in contact with Lucy, Barnett was on the way to get her, he was leaving to get Amy and that no one had managed to get in contact with

Oliver. Jack suggested he go, but I made sure that I went with him as back up. No-one was to be left on their own right now.

We reached Oliver's home, and it was quiet. Deathly quiet. Not even the birds were singing. I felt a lump come to my throat, had we come too late?

We knocked on the door. It creaked open eerily. Jack and I took out our guns with a silent look. We entered the home, Jack going left into the kitchen and I going right.

Nothing.

Nothing.

We head towards the back of the house, before thinking to go upstairs. Nothing out back. Jack had moved ahead of me, as we climbed the stairs. We separated, moving into different bedrooms. A little girl's room, pink splashed all over the walls, Barbie dolls, princesses from Disney littered the floor. And then a deep red. I moved slower, my heart in my throat. I found her. A little princess still in her dress up, I bit back a sob and moved away. I reached the next room, a study by the looks of it, and someone still sat at the computer, I didn't need to get any closer, the red that splattered the computer screen told me everything. Another sob threatened. I moved on. The bedroom was clearly the master bedroom, and the still figure that lay sprawled over the floor, was a woman, and by her looks, matched the little princess in pink bedroom. Another sob, I pushed it aside once more, until I met with Jack. He looked ashen. We had been too late. We heavily went down to the first floor, where we heard a car pull in the driveway, we pointed our guns to the door, Barnett appeared, we slowly lowered the guns and shook our heads. Words would only make this real. They were all dead.

"I have to call this in." I croaked finally. "Did you find-"I couldn't finish the word.

"Yes." Was all Jack said.

I left the house, croaked out that we had a murder into my mobile to the station, forensics would be here shortly, and I hung up. One of us was dead, as well as his family. One of our team members was dead. Because of a mole, because someone had allowed two criminals, two supernatural beings to be free to do this. I saw Amy and Lucy in Barnett's car, and I walked over shaking my head. They broke down into sobs. I felt a sob brewing myself. I fought it until I saw Mary arrive, she saw the look on my face, the two girls in sobs in a car, safe but knew straight away who this was. I pointed inside the house, afraid to speak.

Another department came to take our statements, we were too close to the victim they said and that they would investigate this murder for us. Jack and Barnett appeared a little while later, once they had given their statements, Lucy and Amy had broken out in floods of tears after they had given theirs.

A man down. A good man down. No-one left but us to mourn him and his family. I kept seeing that princess. The blood pooling around her like angel wings. I choked up thinking about her. A little girl cut down, because of her brother being on my team, a life cut short.

The funeral would be held a few days from now, and we were told to take some bereavement leave. We did.

It was the only way to preserve our team member's memory. Oliver. A good teammate who worked hard since he started with us.

I went to a hotel room with Jack, he and I went to pick up some clothes for us both, but we wouldn't be staying at the house. We stopped once before the hotel, to grab cigarettes. The both of us would be smoking a lot in our grief. We split the room, neither of us wanting to be alone.

Once we were in that enclosed space, the both of us broke. Infront of one another. We clutched each other in our grief. When the tears had finished, we wiped our eyes, and grabbed the cigarettes. Luckily for us the hotel had a balcony and we could smoke there. And we smoked, ordered room service as neither of us wanted to leave the room even for a second without the other. With the food we ordered a bottle of whiskey, which we shared straight from the bottle.

Silence.

Lots of the days of our leave we spent in silence. But we didn't need words. We clung to each other every night in the bed, not wanting to leave the other, afraid that if we awoke to the other gone, then something would happen to them while we slept.

We left the hotel room, once to attend the funeral for Oliver and the second to grab more cigarettes. Together. We didn't linger at the after party, showed up for those there celebrating Oliver's life and the lives of his parents and sister. We went back to the hotel room, loosening the clothes that we felt choked the life from us.

Smoked.

When at last words came to us, our throats were hoarse from disuse.

"Mags."

"Jack."

No other words were needed. We jumped into one another's arms and that led to a passionate night for the both of us. We needed the skin on skin, the closeness and the intimacy that we had missed due to our grief.

When we lay beside one another, dressed in the sheet we addressed the elephant in the room.

"Jack." I paused. "How are you now?"

"Ask me again when this is over." He sighed, running a hand through his hair. "I still feel on edge, like someone else is going to be ripped from us." He paused and looked down. "I fear that will be you."

I sat up and leaned on his chest, just enough to show him I was going nowhere.

"I'm not going anywhere, anywhere you go I go." I said softly tracing his jaw. He tensed slightly, and then relaxed into my touch.

"I believe that." He replied softly. "How are you now?" He asked.

"I feel that we failed, that we were up against something we were unprepared for. Even though I thought about it once, I never believed we would be up against the supernatural, as you said. Supernatural does not come into the job description." I heard his heartbeat as I lay on his chest, his arms around me.

"How can we win against such a thing?" He sighed, his hands tracing pictures on my waist.

"I don't think we can." I said. "The only thing that could defeat them is something supernatural and I wouldn't know where to start with that. Or with whom."

He paused. Then as though something struck him, he jumped, causing me to fall off him, onto the bed. He jumped up, pulled on his boxers and grabbed a piece of paper.

"What are you doing?" I queried, wrapping the bedsheets tighter around me. I watched him as he wrote two names down. Placing them on the wall opposite the bed. Then he wrote down more. Placing them underneath, I could see what he was doing. He was using anagrams. Grabbing my phone from the bedside cabinet I typed in using the hotels Wi-Fi and asked for an anagram solver.

"What have you got?" I asked.

"Iris Rouse."

I punched that in. Some nonsense.

"Next?"

"Ric Eluf."

I punched that in and blanched at the name that came up, I shakily said. "Lucifer." Jack and I looked at each other in panic and fear. If it was Lucifer? Who had opened the Gates of Hell? And how the

hell (pun intended) where we going to get them closed again?

I punched in the name Iris Rouse again. I rouse Evil came out. More fear, more horror and more panic ensued.

How were we going to defeat these two? One being who roused evil and one who was the embodiment of evil itself?

Chapter 24

Morale was low, that was a certainty.

We still mourned the loss of Oliver when the call came from above. His empty desk was a reminder of where he had been and who he had been. I was the one to tidy it when I came in. I didn't bin anything but rubbish, we were memorialising him and his family, a little picture of him in the station with some artefacts of his from his desk and on his grave pictures of him and his family, our contribution.

Apparently, we were having someone new join us. We were a little against it, considering that it wasn't long ago that we lost Oliver, but it came above the Chief. We needed a member and member we would have.

Turns out it wasn't so bad, he was youngish, wasn't sure that wasn't even a word, he had long blond hair, startling blue eyes, that held secrets older than his age.

His name was Mikhail Jehovah. I was a little dubious at the name, but he soon integrated himself into the group, putting us all at ease. We all breathed a sigh of relief when he came to help us, not that he had much to help us with. It had all gone quiet, like the calm before the storm. He was well liked, just not by Jack. Jack had become not obsessive but overprotective over me. And although I thought that Mikhail was nice to look at, I was faithful to Jack, and no matter how much I protested that, he was self-conscious every time he worked alongside Mikhail. He had nothing to worry about, as I constantly reminded him, I was going nowhere. My feelings for Jack were growing, more than just liking him. I was beginning to feel that to me, dreaded L-word. I hadn't told him yet; I was waiting for the appropriate time. Not that there was much. He was avoiding me, even when we returned to the Hotel room alone.

I was hurting, I tried to talk to him, when he ignored me and avoided me, I didn't sleep well, and it was beginning to show. It was as though he had stopped caring. It hurt masses. That was for sure. I wanted to end it then, if he was just going to avoid me. I had said this, as I packed my suitcase one day, prepared to leave him half the money for the hotel room we had shared, as I moved to a smaller one and affordable one for me. When he had walked in and saw me packing, preparing to leave, he didn't say anything though. Just watched me. When I had had enough, I confronted him.

"Well?" I even had my hands on my hips. "I am moving to another room; you've been ignoring me since Mikhail started. I have no interest in him, but you are acting as though he has already managed to pilfer me from you. As though I have cheated. It hurts Jack. I have shown him no interest, the only person I love is you!" Then I realised what I said and placed my hands over my mouth. Shock filled me.

He stood still, silent.

I could feel the pinprick of tears in my eyes. When he said nothing, I continued. "Well, then I take that as your answer. I love you but you don't feel the same that is clear. I leave you half the money for this room that we have shared, thank you. I am moving to another room. See you at work. Goodbye Jack." I threw the money on the bed, picked up my suitcase and made to move past him. He threw his arms around my waist. Halting me in my tracks.

"Please Mags, don't leave." He said croakily. "Please."

"But- "I started before he pulled me down onto the floor onto my knees.

"Please." He was crying now. Clutching me tight. "Please don't leave me. I am so sorry."

I patted his back. "I love you Jack. I would not cheat; I am not that sort of woman." And then I forced myself from his arms. "But if you believe that is me, then you don't know me at all." I stood. "Maybe it would benefit us both to have some time apart."

"Mags please!" He begged. I turned and wished I hadn't. I wasn't a cruel woman, but I felt my heart shatter at his actions. My shoulders sagged, I wasn't weak in the slightest, but I loved him, and love makes fools of us all. I put the suitcase down.

"Thank you. Thank you." He took me into his arms and kissed me passionately. I felt him pull me closer. His hands on my hips. "I am sorry Mags." He murmured. I placed my hands on his back as he hugged me.

And as touching as this moment was, it was ruined by our mobiles ringing.

Back to work we went.

Murders had begun happening again.

The first one happened to a young man, he happened to be crossing the street, and he was brutally attacked. It was hard to establish whether the wounds were caused by a gun or a knife. They were that substantial, even Mary with her forensic whizz couldn't discover it. Witnesses we had, they said the killers had carried on hitting him, hurting him, without care that he had been mortally injured. And we had managed to catch the killers. Unusual for us. But it was harder to find whether they had been the ones to kill the poor young man. The only defence they had was "He was Islam innit." He had been of the Muslim faith and it was worrying that racism was beginning to appear in Whitechapel. But then it had been happening for hundreds of years, not just recently.

And this poor young man wasn't the only one. More and more murders were flooding in. It was hard to keep a track of all them.

We decided to one at a time, despite the thoughts of having multiple killers roaming the streets, was a daunting thing. We were hunting, but again much like our previous murders related to a historical crime, we were coming up with nothing. Not even leads, not even suspects.

At least for the poor young man, our suspects were in custody.

For the next victims, that wasn't the case.

They had been poisoned, that much was clear, the only thing they had in common, were they were workers at a plant. This was outside London, for chemical reasons. But somehow, because they lived in Whitechapel, they were in our jurisdiction. They had been found on the streets, having been poisoned and then succumbed to the poison on their way homes, different times and different days. It was still unclear what poison had been used, and forensics were working on that. It was a rare poison, that was clear, until the results came back. They looked as though they had, had a heart attack, but from the colour of their skin, well we had seen poisoned bodies before.

That's what we thought until the next two bodies were found. Again, they had been poisoned, but it was clearly a different poison. These victims had suffered. Truly suffered. They had not only had seizures and cardiac arrest, but family members as well as colleagues had told us that they had been receiving nausea, headaches, feeling unusually weak, having difficulty breathing, and that they had been up until a few days ago, been fit and healthy, in the sense that they were like oxen, very rarely being ill or sick. Highly out of character for them.

Again, forensics were struggling to find the poison and whether it was related to our previous victims. So far, nothing had come to light. It must have meant that they had to have ingested this poison or poisons over a long period of time. We are running out of time to find the poisoner. So that they wouldn't do this to anyone else. Jack suspected the owner of the plant. He said it was because of his nonchalant outlook to the deaths of his workers. He seemed blasé that it had happened and assumed that the four were on drugs of some kind. He refused to make an official statement and got aggressive when we tried to ask him to come to the station. So, in the end we got a warrant and searched his office.

What we found.

Packets of white powder, that Mary told us was strychnine. Rat poison in its powdered form, which small parts had been found in our first two victim's blood. And if that wasn't enough to lock him up the other things we found would have.

Cyanide.

Arsenic.

Thallium, another rat poison.

Taxine, from the yew tree, it can be used for putting in tea or liquids.

Coniine, a poison that is derived from hemlock.

It wasn't just poisons, in their multitudes in his arsenal. It was the flesh, human flesh we had found in a small cooler under the floorboards. He had been killing for some time, disposing of the bodies and cutting them up. He had also been feeding Rouse's meat pie shop. When that closed, he had nothing left to dispose of the bodies, so he had to then resort to letting them fall where they died. Barnett had chalked it up to this plant owner following the Lambeth Poisoner, much like our previous poisoner. However, this one, took the cake. He believed he *was* the Lambeth Poisoner, told us his name was Dr. Thomas Neil Cream, but a background check, proved he was really Harold Byrne, a doctor who was fired because he had been experimenting on his patients rather than curing them. That was a crime.

But that wasn't the worst yet to come.

Chapter 25

We got reports about a body being dumped in the sewer. Jack and I went to investigate. Dressed in overalls, feet gloves and gloves for our hands, we entered the sewers.

At first the smell hit me it was unexplainable, the smell of overripe food, rotting food, human waste all mixed together. Dankness from the glistening walls, the dripping of water and other substances I really didn't want to know about. The water and unknown substances hit against my legs and I was thankful I was wearing overalls. Darkness met us too, the only sources of light hitting us were from cracks in the ceiling, that my mind recognised as manhole covers.

At least if it got into my shoes, I could wash them, but the clothes, my uniform was something I couldn't replace. We hiked, for what seemed like hours but were mere minutes that passed.

Then we came across the body.

Mary was already on the scene. She too was dressed in the overalls. She was also heavily pregnant by this point as well. It must have been extremely nauseating for her, when she was sensitive to smells. I was just about managing with Vaseline up my nostrils to block the smell, but that permeated into the skin on my face. I knew I would be washing extremely closely when I got back to the hotel room. Taking my eyes off the very pregnant Mary, I looked down at the body. Blood covered them, that was sure. It also looked as though it had been nibbled at by rats. And had been decomposing for a little while. It was grotesque. But what was most fascinating in a sense was how the ribcage had been spread open, that took great strength, even a mortician struggled with their instruments on a good day. Clotted blood lined everywhere so it was hard to see with an untrained eye what was missing. And there had to be something missing, why else would the rib cage be open as much as it was.

Mary stood, greeted us, a hand on her swollen belly. "Well, another unusual one. Haven't seen one of these in a while." She looked back down. "The ID in the victim's wallet, found in the back pocket of the jeans, is Harry Wallace. And looked as though he was a plumber, who had been fired recently. We are contacting his last employer to judge when he went missing, family none to speak to. Friends limited, none of them live in London. They've been contacted to identify his body."

"So, what do we think happened to Mr. Wallace?" I asked. Jack nodding in agreement.

"Well, he was obviously dragged down here, died here. From what I can gather. His ribcage was broken into before pulling apart, all while the poor man was still alive. He died instantly once the ribs pierced his lungs and heart." Mary continued, pointing at the ribcage in turn.

"Painful."

"Agonisingly. But, if you look." We did. "The heart, liver and kidneys are missing." We straightened up the smell of decomposing body hitting the Vaseline soaked nostrils. "We have more tests to run when we can get the body back to the lab, to see whether there is anything in his system or how the killer managed to rip open his ribcage."

"Thanks Mary." I said, "Take it easy though yeah??" I pointed at her belly.

"Got to, make sure everything's done before I hand over for my maternity leave." She winked.

I laughed as Jack and I made our way back up into daylight, the sun shining down, blinding us for a few moments on our return to the surface.

On returning to the surface, what happened in the sewers hit me like a tonne of bricks. Someone else had been brutally murdered and I had a flashback to when the Ripper murders started. I almost had a panic attack but focused instead on Jack. He was removing his overalls and wiping the Vaseline out from his nostrils. I smiled as I looked down, removing my own. He really was a great Sergeant and an amazing boyfriend, when he wasn't fast asleep, working hours that we worked was stressful, we only managed to sleep occasionally, that would be less often now we had another case. We returned to the team. Mikhail had settled in well, he had a knack for calming the distressed friends and families, something about his presence. The team accepted, him and now even Jack was warming to him. He was hard at work when we arrived, the preliminary files had come from the forensics team and he was researching our victim. The others were writing on the fresh as a daisy whiteboard, information he had already printed out. Jack and I barely had anything to do, but I walked over and wrote down what we had found out just by talking to Mary. Then we addressed them.

"The victim's ribcage had been forced open while he was still alive." The team winced visibly. "He had been dragged to the sewer, had his heart, liver and kidneys removed while he was alive. The ribs pierced the heart and lungs and he drowned in his own blood." I tried to show no emotion. That was physically hard. "We need to find out his movements before he died, some of which forensics will be doing, but we must do the groundwork." I turned to the team. "Have we found any recent photographs of the deceased?"

"Yes Ma'am." Amy said, holding out a picture. "He had one on his Facebook page, we managed to find him."

"Good work team." I said smiling. "Get out there and see if anyone recognises him so that we can follow his movements before he was dragged to the sewer."

"Aye, aye Ma'am" They saluted as one. And I laughed.

"Alright, no need for that, just get to it." They dispersed.

Jack and I were left in the room, I stood, arms crossed staring at the whiteboard, another picture posted on the whiteboard. I was sure I had seen his face before, but where?

"What you are thinking?" Jack asked, standing beside me, adopting the same stance.

"I've seen his face before. But I can't place him." I tapped my chin thoughtfully.

"Yeah, I have too." Jack's face became a frown. "Have we interviewed him?"

I shook my head. "Not sure, we may have done, there's been so much death…" I paused. "They all start to merge after a while."

Jack hummed in reply. We stood for some time, just looking at the picture.

"I think I will have a look in our records Mags, see if we have interviewed him and what for." He touched my shoulder.

"Ok Jack." I smiled at him. "See you here when you finish."

"Don't leave without me." He said. "When forensics call."

"Wouldn't dream of it." I said. He left and I stared a little more intently at the photograph. There was something in the background, but it was fuzzy.

The phone rang in my office, startling me out of my intensity. I rushed to answer it.

"D.I. Abberline." I said.

"Ma'am, you need to get down to forensics asap." Came the voice on the other end. I thanked them and hung up. Stopping on the way down, to grab Jack. We entered the now familiar laboratory that was now like a second home, with the amount of dead bodies we had encountered.

Mary greeted us, sitting in a chair. "Sorry for not standing to greet you." She apologised.

We waved her off. "What have you found?" We asked in unison. Mary chuckled.

"You spend so much time together, your beginning to become twins."

We laughed. Mary knew about our personal as well as our professional relationship, apparently, she had 'shipped' us for years.

"What did you find?" I asked, with Jack nodding beside me.

"Well, they did a number on Mr. Wallace." She said. "Not only did they take his organs, they cut off his genitals." I heard Jack wince loudly beside me.

"To what end though?" I asked.

"That I don't know." Mary shook her head slowly. "They took the genitals as a trophy of some kind. The organs, I have no idea unless the are running a black-market organ donation service?"

"We could start with that." Jack said, he still winced. "black market organ donation. Then we can look at other avenues, we can ask Barnett."

I nodded, we thanked Mary and left to go back to the team room, where a ruffled looking Barnett stood at his desk, history repeated itself as we had found, he had immediately begun searching the minute the call came in regarding how the body had been found, the organs, the opening of the rib cage, all in the preliminary report sent to us.

"You've been busy." I said to Barnett.

"Yep. Jack, Mags, I found quite a few things. Cults harvesting organs in the 1900's, cults stealing genitals as trophies," He winced, and Jack winced for a third time. "People ripping open rib cages..." He looked up. "What do you want to start with?"

"Try the cult with harvesting organs." I said, "I can always look at the cults stealing genitals, especially if it is painful for you two."

They nodded. Each of us took a file and read, making a few notes, talking our thoughts out loud to one another as we found something. Then that idea would be crossed out and started over again. We had a good system going until Max and Lucy came running into the room.

"Mags!" They shouted. "We found him!" They panted breathlessly, excited that they had managed to track down the victim.

"He lives in a small flat off Ratcliffe, he was next door to the second family when they were murdered. He had done the plumbing for them once; they had become good neighbours and friends. Before he disappeared, he had been drinking at the Ten Bells." Lucy said in a rush. Links to our previous cases and the Ripper one in the 1800's.

Max nodded.

"Great work you two." I smiled, "Go and add that to the board, will you? We are looking for historical references."

"Oooh, could there be one?" Lucy asked.

"More than likely." I said. "All our others had some connection of some kind. Why wouldn't this one be different?"

They hummed in agreement.

Soon we were all putting our noses to the grind, shouting things across the room when our final two members arrived.

"We did it!" Amy shrieked. "He had been at the Ten Bells, then he went to St Patrick's Cemetery, where the family were murdered in their home, he then went on a Ripper Tour, and ended up in the street above the sewer, someone saw him as they let their cat out." Mikhail nodded, a small smile on his face.

We cheered, clapping the two on the backs at their hard work.

As they celebrated, I watched my thoughts flickering to the fact that several of the places our victim attended were either a past case of history or one of ours today. That was strange.

It also seemed coincidental. Had he been following us? Was he a closet fan, god did we need them, but still… something was off? Unless it was a way to get our attention? Again, pure coincidence.

We had last movements, I would retrace his steps, just not the Tour. I had, had enough of the Ripper to last me a lifetime. I would go to the sights, the cemeteries, and our last cases. I would go alone. The team would never be too far though, at least one would be nearby. Jack wasn't too happy about that and had begged me, on his knees begging back in the hotel room, that I didn't need to do it. That one of the men could do it, but I wanted to. If it stopped the people doing this, then it meant it would end faster. And as I told him, it meant I could retire. I had, had enough of being a police officer. That much was true. He had slumped in shock when I had said that. I worried he had bumped his head as he fell, but he soon sat up and questioned me. Was that really what I wanted? Wouldn't I miss it? What did that mean for him and me?

I had gotten down on my knees, with some difficulty, and took his face in my hands, it meant that he wouldn't need to worry about me on the job anymore, that was what I wanted, I had done enough. I would miss fighting the criminals with him and the team, but not the murder side of it. Him and me? That was easy! I still wanted to be with him, even if it meant worrying about him instead of the other way around.

He had taken my hands, pulled me close and said if that was my decision, he supported me one hundred percent. It would be when this big case was complete, the chief had already been made aware of this. He was wholehearted behind me.

Despite that I worked hard alongside my team, who didn't, aside from Jack know about my retirement. They seemed pleased with work they had produced, but we still couldn't find why he had been taken, he had no debts overpaid, he didn't owe anyone anything. There was nothing contributing to why he had been killed, none. None we could find that they could decipher. Neither could I.

That was when the next body came in.

Another young person murdered. In the same way as Harry Wallace.

He had been murdered in the same way. Ribcage torn open, heart, lungs and kidneys taken, but they still couldn't decipher how they had managed to force the ribcage open so neatly. Unless there were multiple people as the killers? That was the only thing that made sense. Multiple people attacking one person, ripping open the ribcage and tearing out the organs that they needed. It would also explain how someone who was built like an ox and who had the muscles that made them seem like a sinewy tiger. Surely one person, would not have been overtaken by another so easily? It made more and more sense as we spoke about it, were we dealing with a cult after all?

But how would we catch them? When we had found no hide nor hair of any of them? They had vanished like ghosts, catching and dispelling like mist. No one has seen anyone covered in blood roaming the streets after the murders, and that amount of blood would have been immense as Mary constantly told us. There was a lot of blood and fluid within the chest cavity. Anyone delving into it, would be covered in blood. Anyone ripping open a ribcage would also be covered in blood and fluid. Along with bone fragments. But we had found nothing. We were frantic now.

Trying to find the killers before they struck again, but we had no idea who we were hunting or why they were killing these people. I had even done my walk around the victims last moments on earth, and I wasn't targeted. It made no sense. The team were beginning to delve into urgency, they were as hungry to find this person or people.

What was the significance of the heart, liver and kidneys? Why just them?

Barnett had managed to cultivate and investigate what would those organs be used, everything from the Egyptians to modern day Hinduism. Egyptians also was sure that they would need the stomach and the brain on their journeys to the afterlife. Hinduism said that donating organs meant selflessness. That didn't make sense either. The brain and other organs hadn't even been touched. Genitals yes, brain and stomach no. Was it lust? And everything to do with being lustful? Did we have a religious cult on our hands? I had hoped this was not true. Barnett found in his research, someone from Australia, who had taken male victims, stabbed them in a similar fashion to our Ripper, and had cut their genitalia from their body. But that didn't fit. But at least we are looking at all options.

We were running of time.

There were going to be more and if we couldn't stop it more people will die. More innocent lives would be in danger. Mikhail, also seemed more ruffled than ever, dashing out to care for his mother, who was sick and dying. His stress levels were affecting all of us, and ours affecting his when he had already had so much on his plate.

It didn't help that lights began to flicker again, faulty electrics. The station was refusing to get it fixed, mainly because it was just our room that was being affected the most. There was no explanation from the power company, apparently everything connected properly. There was no explanation.

Max decided he would go on the hunt; he went down to the lower levels of the station. Lucy went with him. The lights flickered eerily down there as well. It wasn't until they found water leaking that they found the reason. Someone had stuck nails into the main water pipe, causing the dripping and the electrics down there were being affected. They came up to let the main desk know and to let us and the rest of the team know as well. Who had stuck the nails there in the first place though? They wouldn't have just stuck themselves in on their own.

Sabotage.

Damage.

Impairment.

Incapacitation.

That's what it was.

On a whim, I wandered one day on a break, we all needed them every so often, I wandered to St Patrick's Cemetery. I stood in front of Mary Jane Kelly's grave. Asked for her help. Was unsure who else could help. We were on our own, and if a spirit could help, well we were open to all sorts.

In theory.

In practice, we relied on more reliable sources of investigation and support.

Until, the next murder happened. This time in the sewer, I didn't look at the body, instead I looked around us. How were they getting the body here? How did they get away with no one seeing the blood, fluid and bone fragments? Unless... they moved through the sewer. That was the next move. We looked at a plan of the sewers under Whitechapel. Locating where the three victims had been murdered.

Mikhail noticed it before we did.

"Churches." He said, pointing to each of the churches on the map. "They are all near churches." Then we saw what he meant. All the meaning came back. Religion had a small part to play in it, so in teams we wandered near those churches, hoping that we would find someone. I had teamed up with Mikhail on this occasion. Jack and Barnett went and looked at another.

Mikhail was very good at blending into the crowd. Me not so much even in plain clothes. My hair gave me a way a lot of the time, people moved out of the way when they saw me, so Mikhail decided to walk ahead of me, and I followed. He took the lead on this one. When he stopped I did too. He spoke to someone who pointed up the street beside the church, he thanked them and came back to talk to me.

"Apparently there has been a group, they have been preaching about the end of the world, handing out flyers. A cult by the sounds of it. They believe that the end is coming, and Whitechapel will be the place where the Devil will take hold." Mikhail explained.

"Shall we go and check them out?" I asked him. He nodded. He seemed worried though. Then his smile appeared on his face.

"I'm ok Ma'am." He said, I swore he read my mind sometimes. It was uncanny. I couldn't believe it, a possible lead though despite the obstacles we had.

From a distance we saw them. Handing out flyers and preaching about the end of days. How Whitechapel would be the Devil's playground... then when they moved, so did we.

We followed from a distance. Kept them in our sights. Followed them until they disappeared.

"How? Where?" I stammered. I felt anger, pure undiluted anger, rise in me. We were so close and again like mist they escaped through our fingers.

We had to back track to the station. The others had come across the same situations at all the churches. All members of this so-called cult had disappeared like they were made of mist, like ghosts. But we knew where they were. In and around those churches during the day, looking for people to convert and bring to their hideaway. One of us had to get in there.

Amy offered and I shook my head. They would refuse her, especially since her transition. They didn't accept her in the Bible, and neither would those cultists. Lucy offered. We were all reluctant to let her, but it seemed the only option. She seemed innocent enough, pure enough for the cultists. So, we let her. Though someone was always with her, at a distance hidden keeping surveillance.

It seemed that our luck had run out. They seemed to have gone to ground. Something had spooked them. Or where they planning their next kill? So where were the body parts, surely, they would spoil or rot?

Chapter 26

We had to pause in our investigation the group had gone underground.
But that didn't mean that we weren't working behind the scenes.

Barnett had dug out some information on Doomsday cults throughout history. The Family, the Falun Gong cult in China, The Order of the Solar Temple, all based around different beliefs, from the religious harmless to harmful. It seemed our cult was a mix of The Family and Falun Gong cult in China. They believed that the Rapture was upon us, and they were harvesting people they believed were sinners. That linked to genitalia, men were the instigators usually of lust, though in the Bible, it was Eve who was the first sinner, so it was a surprise that they weren't attacking women. Unless they were the opposite, believing that men were the ones who had the most sin of lust. Thus, removing the genitalia, prevents them from committing that sin, and therefore being allowed into the kingdom of heaven? We wouldn't know until we had the group in front of us to question. This rate, that wasn't an option. But we still went out, in plains clothes, so we wouldn't attract attention.

I did have a thought about the organs that were being removed. Was the cult eating them? Were they someone ingesting their fellow man, to believe that what their victims had, such as courage, wit, strength would thus flow into them? When I brought my suspicions to Barnett, he brought up a file on the Chijon family in 1993, who killed their rich victims and cooked their flesh for that same belief. It seemed plausible to me that's what they were doing as we had no reports about rotting flesh or cooked flesh or anything similar. But where were they doing all of this? They had to have a base, a home where they all lived. For the number of people who were on the streets recruiting, it had to have been a large area. Plus, the ones we hadn't seen.

It made no sense. We had no names though and that was a thing we needed to even get started. That was until we had a shy and somewhat unwilling informant come forward. The young lady stood awkwardly at the front desk, who had called us telling we had someone wanting to talk to us.

Jack and I approached her. She had long brunette hair, dressed in a long skirt that hung below her knees, a blouse and crucifix around her neck. Her eyes were a chocolate brown, and right now they were filled with fear and worry. Like she didn't want to be there, but she had to.

"Hello?" I said tentatively. "And what's your name Miss?" I asked.

"Angelina." She said quietly, she was fidgeting.

I noticed and asked if we could have an interview room so she would be able to talk to us in absolute privacy. She seemed a little bit more at ease as we took her not to an interrogation room but to a little room, where she could relax more, as we locked the door behind her.

"Anything you tell us Angelina, is confidential." Jack said, giving the woman a small smile.

"Thank you." She started to play with the crucifix. "I didn't want to come, but I felt you needed to know. I think that the person that you are looking for used to be in my congregation."

"And what makes you think this Angelina?" I asked, concern in the tone of my voice.

She shifted uncomfortably. "The flyers, I recognised the way of speech. It was Adam. Adam Hamilton."

"And do you think it's him?" Jack probed gently.

She took some time before answering and we let her. Admitting to the someone being someone you knew, being a potential killer, well it was a life changing thing.

"Because he came to our priest and asked for his opinion on some of the book of Revelation scriptures." She said softly. "The priest told him, what was in the book of revelation was what was written, for our faith and belief, there is no interpretation. Adam grew angry." She paused, her hands fidgeting with her crucifix.

"It's alright Angelina, take as much time as you need." I said softly, offering a warm smile. "Our faith is something that we live by, right?"

"You're of the faith?" She asked.

"I was raised, it I admit I was shaken off the path a while, but after the things I have seen, I wander back to it when I need it. And I know that God will forgive me." I replied. "God is forgiving after all."

She nodded, then as if that helped, she sat up a little straighter, grew bolder as she continued. "He grew angry that the priest didn't interpret the book of revelations the way he did, and vowed that when the end days came, he would be the one with the ones that followed him, they would be the ones accepted into heaven in the rapture, and the rest of us would have to wait until judgement day."

I allowed what Angelina told us to sink into my head.

"So, what did Adam do after that?" Jack asked. I knew Jack wasn't religious, however he understood and sympathised with the young woman in front of us.

"He grew followers within the congregation, and they left with him. It was a large amount, and I fear for their immortal souls. What Adam preached." She shuddered. "I am pretty sure that he would have been smote from God with his words. I fear he is creating another Sodom. And I fear for my friends who follow him." She finished. "He spoke about taking in the strength of those who are pure by eating their flesh and removing the reproductive organs to prevent lust in the future."

Was it as easy as that?

"Where is Adam now?" Jack asked.

"I am not sure, he sold his home and moved, he said he needed a big space for his congregation. But chances are if he believes in what he does, he will be underground or hidden somewhere where there aren't a lot of people." Angelina replied. "I was friends with his son. His son was afraid of what his father preached, but he has to do what he says."

"How old is this son?" I asked, if anyone could get us in, the son could.

"Seventeen, eighteen in a few weeks." Angelina replied. "I hope he is ok." She added.

"We'll find him Angelina, what's the son's name?" Jack asked, giving a reassuring smile.

"Joshua." Angelina replied.

We thanked the young lady for coming to us, she had been a huge help and we would find her friend and bring him back to her and away from his father's influence. But we still had to find them. We began looking into properties that Adam Hamilton had been interested in. The team went to estate agents, asking with Adam's picture. Most hadn't seen him or spoken to him. Perhaps he had gone private?

We began then to investigate private properties. None of which had been looked at by someone named Adam Hamilton.

I feared for young Joshua Hamilton. If he didn't want to follow his father, who knew what the father would do, if he saw his son as a betrayer.

I didn't want to believe that someone would kill their own son, but even in the Bible, Abraham almost killed his until an angel stopped him. What would stop someone from doing the same with these cult ideas of the end coming. What torture lay ahead for them? What was even happening? I hoped that none of those that followed Adam had been hurt, injured or killed because of what he believed in.

Mikhail and Lucy went out the following day, pretending that they were looking for religion in the churches. They acted well, and from a distance we watched as some of the cult saw them. That was the idea, to get the two noticed. They would then continue going to the churches, seeking religion until one of the cult members would approach them. The cult was hesitant, however no one sought them out.

We were no nearer to finding their location either. Most of us worked overtime, without pay, to try and find this hideaway. Looking at warehouses that had underground storage, to looking for people camping out outside of London, that was a fluke thought, but it didn't sit right. We hunted. We pursued this group with everything we had. We tracked, we hounded, we even trailed the cult members where we could. Each time the disappeared without a trace. We were becoming alarmed that nothing was working out for us.

Mikhail and Lucy weren't too blame. I was. I was leading this team into a pit of despair. With no way out. When many of the team were out or working hard, I would close my office door and sit with my head on my desk. And like a deer in headlights, when someone knocked, I would be up and alert. I was glad that after this case was finished, I would then be retiring. Too much stress like this was bad for the body. I was beginning to not sleep and have insomnia. A headache formed constantly behind my eyes. But I didn't let anyone see that it was causing me pain. I carried on. Like always.

The last time we went out, as a team we decided that if we didn't find them then we would have to resort to knocking on places with search warrants and demand to be allowed in.

That was until a very nervous young man came into the station, asking only to speak to me.

"Are you D.I Abberline?" He asked, his eyes darting all over the place.

I nodded. "And you are?"

"Joshua Hamilton." He whispered. "My friend Angelina told me that you were trying to stop my father?"

"Joshua? Well we are glad to see you are alive. We were all worried about you." I whispered. "Shall we go and talk in private? Just let me get the Sergeant." I nodded at Jack who was watching anxiously.

We took him to the same interview room; we took Angelina into.

"What you tell us will be completely confidential, and we can put you into hiding." I continued.

He seemed relieved straight away. "I never believed in what my dad preached. He scared me, just like he's scared a few others. We follow him out of fear and well he's my dad." He shrugged. "It wasn't until one day he asked me to go with him and catch some meat, I thought he meant to go to the butchers. But I was wrong, when he killed that person, I didn't know who he was anymore. But I couldn't get out. I was too far in." He began to shake. "I went out one day with one of the other members who are afraid and petrified of my dad. We managed to lurk around the church, where we used to go, and I left a note for the priest to give to Angelina. That's why she came here to speak to you. I asked her to. And when I could escape, I would come to you myself." He paused.

It was a lot to take in. So, not all the members were aware of how they got the meat they ate. That was reassuring.

"Names Joshua of the people who are petrified?" I asked. Jack nodded, ready to take them down.

"Well- "Hesitated.

"So, when we find them, we won't arrest them officially, it means that they can be saved and recognised as being threatened and coerced." Jack added. "That way, they like you can be kept safe,"

Joshua nodded and began to reel off names. Many of which he said where his friends. They had also seen his father kill an innocent, and I knew all these poor young people had seen things that they would never be able to unsee. And they would more than likely be in therapy for, for a foreseeable future.

When Joshua had finished with the names, we then asked him where they had been hiding. He shakily told us that they lived underneath one of the abandoned churches in Whitechapel, near Christchurch, in catacombs that had been modified for them to live in until the Rapture happened. He pointed to the place on a map when Jack fetched one, and even pointed out how to get in. We had hit a lucky break. We thanked Joshua, and we hid him. He hid with Mikhail for the time being, he had paused looking at Mikhail for some reason and then smiled. Crossed himself and left happily.

We worked out a plan, we would send a van for those who were directly involved in the killing and that included Joshua's father Adam, and a separate van for the young people and children to take them to safety, the ones not directly involved or afraid. We would then take the ones who were involved to a separate location, where half would go into another van. I wasn't making any mistakes this time. No-one would be getting away, not this time.

Chapter 27

Joshua was right.

In the catacombs they did hide. We had scoped the place out before we were going to enter. No surprises. We had no idea if they were armed, as Joshua wasn't allowed into those meetings. Apparently too young to know about weaponry but old enough to be able to kill someone.

They had no one on guard. It was quite worrying, but all the better for us.

We stalked them, all wearing night gear, so we blended into the catacombs, armed, bullet proof jackets under our clothes, vans at the ready outside hidden ready for when I gave the word. My team were stashed around the catacombs, turns out there were multiple entrances, through the sewers. I separated from Jack, he didn't like it, but knew I would be safe with Barnett.

We were like wolves, travelling in a pack searching for our prey. Then we heard them, the chanting. Prayer. They were praying. I was surprised that Adam hadn't thought about his son, who had vanished.

In position we waited.

And waited.

And waited. Then I gave the signal.

Like a wave we moved as one.

Arrested them on sight, many surrendered to us, their arms in the air. I knew those were the ones who Joshua said were petrified. The ones that didn't, well they fought back, and we used measurable force to take them down. They had guns, for a group that relied on nonviolence, they had a lot of weapons, and I knew I took a bullet to the arm at one point, the adrenaline pumping through my system until they had all been rounded up and brought to the surface. Most of them blinked, having been down in those catacombs for a long time.

We herded them into the appropriate places, when Jack came over, a huge grin on his face as he saw me, until he saw the blood. He dragged me over to an ambulance, who had arrived as a precaution. They cleaned the wound and I felt right as rain. We made sure the vans knew where they were headed, and made our way back to the station, ready to celebrate.

We had done it.

For once everything had gone to plan, we had suspects on their way to the station, the ones who were petrified were safe.

We had done a good job, and I overheard a few talking about when the suspects arrived and were booked, they were going for a drink in the Bells.

I had agreed it was a good idea, but I had a lot of paperwork to make sure was done, before I could go home. Perks of being a D.I.

Jack offered to stay and help, but I waved him away to go and have a drink, assuring him once the paperwork was done, I would join them.

The first van of suspects arrived; the ones who had been separated from Adam Hamilton. They had yet to arrive.

When my phone rang, I was knee deep in the first batch of paperwork from the first lot of arrests, ready to start on the second one and hopefully be able to celebrate more with the team.

"D.I.Abberline." I said into the mouthpiece, while trying to finish the report I was writing. The news that I received shocked me to my very core. I dropped the phone in utter shock. It the desk with a loud clunk.

The van holding our cult leader and his close followers had crashed. And had soon been engulfed in black smoke, it is moving through the sky like a dark spirit as I sat there.

I was glad that I had moved half into another van. My question was how did the van crash in the first place?

I sent Mikhail to the place of the crash, and he nodded and willingly went. He went to take statements and to see how the van had crashed in the first place. Slowly, I picked up the phone, that hung by its cord and placed it back on the handset. The team, when I told them were gobsmacked. We had heard of things like this happening on television shows, but not in real life.

I waited for the verdict from Mikhail, telling the others to go. I would join them later. I had to deal with the rest of the paperwork, and despite the crash, we still had half of the cult in the station. That was something to celebrate at least.

When Mikhail returned, covered in a tar like substance, which I believed to be the smoke. I was surprised.

"You ok?" I asked him, with a frown.

"The smoke was thick, the car had crashed into wall, the radiator exploded. There was no way to save them." He shook his head sadly. "None of them would have survived."

"How did it crash?" I asked, handing him one of my wet wipes I kept in the desk, so he could clean his face and hands.

"Someone said they had seen a woman in the middle of the road, the van swerved and hit the wall, the woman vanished as if she was air." Mikhail added, gladly able to rid the soot from his face and hands.

I sat down, heavily.

The news wasn't great.

Mikhail sank into the chair opposite, looking as weary as I felt.

I groaned. The pain in my arm, shot through my veins like a fire, I was overdoing it.

I told Mikhail to go, and we could reconvene tomorrow, to meet the others at the pub, and that I would be along once I started the reports for the crash and the reports from the second arrests who never arrived. He begrudgingly left. Giving me a second glance, as I pulled the mouse and the keyboard. He said before leaving. "If you're not there in two hours, he would come back and walk me to the pub, or Jack would. It still wasn't safe on the streets for a woman at this time of night." And left.

I worked solidly for two hours, and as promised, finished the reports for the arrests and got half way through the reports for the crash, before sighing, rubbing my eyes, locking my computer, standing, grabbing my coat, turning off the lights in my office, the team room and then locked the door. I stretched outside, hearing the pops from my shoulder and back, then the fire spread through my arm again. I hissed. I wasn't used to being injured on the job. I had completely forgotten about the bullet wound.

I exited the station, rang Jack, who didn't answer, rang Mikhail and said that I would have a cigarette before heading to the pub, where I would meet them. I joked and said that they better have a whiskey with my name on it when I arrived. Then I sparked my cigarette while standing outside the station.

I stood there, relaxing. Something I hadn't done in a while and thought about everything that had happened since a year ago when the Ripper appeared. The team and I had come so far in such a short period of time. Smoke unfurled from my mouth like a dragon. I started to walk as soon as my cigarette was lit properly, and began making my way to the pub.

The empty streets of Whitechapel echoed my footsteps back to me. Every so often you would hear drunken shouts, sirens of fellow police officers keeping the peace from the drunks and the criminals, doors slamming, windows being closed. Then silence.

The streetlamps sent orange and yellow glows onto the dark cement I walked on. I walked past Christchurch pausing only for a moment. The I carried on.

Silence again for a time. And then I felt someone behind me. I turned, there was no one there. Thinking that it would be quicker, I turned to pass through the cemetery near the station, it was quicker, and it was eerily quiet. The odd warning hoot of an owl, the wind rustling the leaves on the trees and the shadows casting figures onto the grass around me. I tightened my grip on my coat, having stomped my cigarette out long ago, pulling it closer around me as though a chill had run down my spine. I longed for another source of light, and as though it had been summoned the moon burst through the grey dyed clouds. It gave me a silver light and I followed it, a beacon guiding me to my end point. Darkened shadows, appeared longer, as though they were reaching out for me with their soot armed fingers. The tree's branches looked as though they were too reaching for me. To stop me or to help me, I was uncertain.

Then the crunch hit my ears, it was loud in the silence. I paused, glancing around me. No-one seemed to be there, I looked under my own feet and sighed. It was me.

A stick stood broken in half under my foot. I gently kicked it aside and carried on. I heard a ping from my pocket, seeing a message from Jack, I smiled and responded, telling him I was on my way. He didn't need to come and rescue me from the paperwork. As I looked up, I walked a little further. The journey seemed to take longer than I had thought, was I lost? I couldn't be, I had travelled this way many times before.And it had taken less time then, it was probably because I was on my own, in the dark and I had just had a massive shock.

The iron gates were in sight. I sighed with relief, not that long left. I could almost taste the beads of whiskey, hear my team laughing and joking with one another, the loudness of drinkers in the pub, the jukebox screaming its tunes, and Jack's arm around my shoulders, laughing about taking my time.

Another crunch sounded behind me.

A fox or a badger on the nightly hunt. I thought, never for once thinking someone was following me.

A Dark shadow.

I smiled again, then when I saw the shadow that stood in-front of me, the smile faltered, and my vision went black. My last vision was of Jack's face a smile, as he waited for me.

Chapter 28

Jack's Point of View.

It was odd.

Maggie should have been here by now.

I checked my watch. She said she was on her way, and she wasn't one to tell lies, I bet she got distracted like she sometimes did. Maybe she made a quick stop on the way to grab something to eat?

I checked my phone, stopping outside with Amy, who wanted a cigarette, looking up and down the street packed with people from the pub for Maggie.

"Still not here?" Amy asked.

"No." I said, frowning at my phone. "She said she was on her way, and that was about ten minutes ago. But if she had run to grab food, she would have messaged me or rang me."

"Maybe, her battery has died?" Amy suggested. "Or she had to stop and help someone? You know what Mags is like."

"I do." I said softly. That was one of the reasons why I loved Mags. Yes, I loved her. I was planning on asking her to marry me tonight. I had to. I didn't want to be without her. She was a light in my life. I didn't know what I would do without her. Amy offered me the rest of her cigarette, complaining that it had gotten cold suddenly.

I took it gratefully, happy to have something to do while I kept my eyes peeled for the love of my life to appear. I was nervous, I wanted to ask her to marry me in front of the team, I felt in my pocket for the small box that I had scrimped and saved for since I had met my first girlfriend, Maggie being far different from her.

When the cigarette was finished and Maggie still hadn't arrived, I stomped it out and went inside, the air, had indeed turned chilly, and more than the smoke came from my lungs. I went inside, weaving through the crowd where I reached the team.

"Anyone else heard from Mags?" I asked. When they shook their heads, I saw Mikhail check his phone.

"Nothing since she tried to ring me about thirty minutes ago." He muttered. "Shall I go and see if I can find her?" He asked looking at me. There was something in his eyes, but it flickered out before I could focus on it further. I nodded, thinking perhaps she had stopped longer to have her cigarette, or even stopped to have a second. The news of the crash of the vans had hit her hard. I didn't blame her in the slightest. Her job was stressful, and the fact she was retiring after this case, was another reason to celebrate, to celebrate Maggie's time with us. It would be sad to see her leave the team, but if she agreed to be my wife, then I would go home to her everynight.

That thought, made me a little more nervous, butterflies in my stomach. I knew I had a smile on my face though. I couldn't wait.

The others, knew about the plan, they were excited for us and had been waiting for this moment for a while. Even Mary, at home was waiting anxiously for the news by the phone.

We still waited.

It was agonising.

I was beginning to wonder if something had happened. If it had why hadn't she called us? My fingers danced on the table, around my beer.

Soon, it was enough to make all of us worry.

We had heard nothing.

Lucy even rang the station, they said she had left over an hour ago. Lucy thanked them and hung up. Worry for Maggie began to niggle in my stomach, and it twinned on everyone's faces.

They all began to ring her mobile. But it was either switched off or went straight to voicemail.

I wondered, had she gone back to the hotel room, because her phone had died? But then she would have used the phone in the room to call.

I was beginning to panic.

Something had to have happened.

But what?

Then my phone rang, to the point where it startled me, I answered it shakily.

"Sergeant Summers." I said.

"Sir, there's been a murder. I tried to ring D.I. Abberline but couldn't get a hold of her."

"Thanks. Where?"

When he said the cemetery fifteen minutes away, I wondered for a moment whether Maggie had seen it happen and was busy dealing with the person who had been murdered and was about to call us any second. I hung up urgently just in case. After a while I sighed, told the team to contact Mikhail and tell him to meet us in the cemetery near the pub, we had to work.

We made our way wearily, stretching as we walked. A small group that we were, we still took up a great deal of the pathway. Asking people to move aside, as we went past, as we were now on official police business.

The wrought iron gates appeared, the worry for Maggie still knotted my stomach, and then entering the cemetery, I realised, there was no sound. I looked around me, concerned.

The air was still frigid. The shadows seemed to beckon us, and something ran down my spine. I wasn't superstitious but something was now beginning to not make sense. The moon then hid as though she wanted to avert her eyes from what she had witnessed.

The air froze in my lungs and I stopped short. A dark mass lay, a finger pointing to a grave. Our murder.

We were the first ones on the site, so we had to wait for forensics. I kept staring at that dark mass. It seemed familiar, but I disbelieved what my gut was telling me. I didn't want to believe it.

When Mary appeared, and took one look at my grim face, she too took a long look at the mass. I didn't want to speak, the words caught in my throat. I couldn't speak, I would choke.

She patted me on the shoulder and went and did her job.

I did mine, the team had already spread out. Looking for a phone, a wallet, anything to tell us who this poor victim was.

I joined them; I didn't want to hang around. When Maggie got here, I would scold her for her absence and not answering her phone. Mikhail was missing too.

That's when a glint, caught my eye. A broken sword, that looked like it was antique. A smear of black soot nearby, and a white feather.

I didn't think much of it when a cry sounded from my left. Amy had fainted. Lucy went over to check she was alright and then she too crumpled to the floor. Barnett and I shared a look. We ran straight there, unsure what they had found.

A small rectangular shape sat there.

I knew that shape, had seen it many times. A strangled cry escaped from my throat and Barnett shouted. "No!"

I ran back to Mary; she would tell me it wasn't true.

It wasn't.

It wasn't her.

It couldn't be…

One look at Mary's face however told me the truth. I turned away, I couldn't…but why…how?

"I'm sorry Jack." Mary whispered, I could hear the tears in her own eyes and mine threatened to spill.

"It's not her." I shook my head. "I- "

Mary gathered me into her arms, I crumpled to the floor, with her holding me.

Numb.

I cried. I cried as my heart shattered into a thousand pieces. She was gone!

The small box fell from my pocket, opening and landing by her outstretched finger, a hand that would never wear it. It's glinting sparkles glistening in the gleam from the lights around her like a halo.